Murder Travels In Threes

by

Sigrid Vansandt

ISBN-13: 9781540403643

To my mother, Kay.

Thank you for sharing wonderful books, comedic stories and, of course, your indefatigable sense of adventure with me. Your insights, love, humor and devotion made this book possible.

Love you!

Table of Contents

Copyright Information

This work was previously published under the title "A Debt Is Finally Paid" by Sigrid Vansandt.

Cover Design by Jenny McGee

See more of Jenny's work at **artistjennymcgee.com**

Under tower and balcony,
By garden-wall and gallery,
A gleaming shape she floated by,
Dead-pale between the houses high.
-Alfred, Lord Tennyson

PREFACE

A FULL AUTUMN MOON'S STEADY gaze illuminated the dark, slow moving water of the quiet canal. No evening pedestrians or cyclists made their way home along the tow path skirting the canal's edge saving the peaceful nighttime ambience from human noise. A mechanical humming from a tethered narrowboat's generator switched on long enough to start a water pump working in its hull but its interruption was brief.

The river's surface pulsated and flickered with silver threads of light and the occasional ripple effect emanating from the settling of another falling autumn leaf testified to the far reaching impact one body can have upon another. Perhaps the truer message awaited the leaf down river as it was folded into the flotsam collecting along the withering and decaying vegetation of the bank.

Cold and persistent, the wind blowing inland from the North Sea played among the buildings lining the canal, skipped across the flowing water and howled a mournful tune as it squeezed through the arches of one of the old stone bridges spanning the River Trent outside of Nottingham. The only other sounds came from the softly sung nighttime melody of the toads accompanied by the raspy chirps of crickets snug in their homes in the tall hardy weeds and grasses not yet dead from the autumn frosts.

Something floated and bumped against the embankment where slender river reeds grew long. A weeping willow tree's graceful limbs waltzed with the meandering current, lightly brushing the top of a human body as it floated past. Water bugs skated between the reeds and across the face of a woman upturned and floating lifeless in the river's tender arms. Canal water filled her open mouth while a small spider crawled onto her cheek using her as a ferry to better habitat down river.

The body was becoming lodged and tangled among the grasses. The silver light from the moon's glow touched her long, curly golden hair as it radiated out from her head giving the illusion of a fiery, undulating crown. As the night edged toward the dawn, ice formed on the exposed skin of the floating corpse sealing her open, staring eyes into frozen orbs. No tears for the lovely thing wrapped in nature's bowery of limbs, leaves and debris. Understanding the ebb and flow of life and death, the river kindly washed them all away.

CHAPTER 1

Marsden-Lacey, Yorkshire, England
Present Day

"WE'VE GOT GYPSIES!" ED GRIMSY bellowed as he stamped into The Traveller's Inn on a crisp, early autumn afternoon in Marsden-Lacey.

Everyone turned, blinked and stared at Old Grimsy as he was called by most people. He flung a fiver down on the bar and Luther Pendergast, the owner and bartender at The Traveller's, poured Grimsy his usual and handed it to him.

"What you going on about Grimsy?" Luther asked.

"I'm telling you," Grimsy warned, "the gypsies are coming down the canal. Three boats. Children, old hags and pipe smoking men and women. Real hair-braiding, thieving gypsies. Headed this way. Won't be long before we're cleaned out of our valuables and our livestock stolen."

He ended his diatribe with a melodramatic crescendo without making direct eye contact with anyone while taking his first swig from his glass. It would take some time for the audience to digest the news.

The pub was ministering to the social and nutritional needs of its patrons which for a typical Marsden-Lacey afternoon meant somewhere in the neighborhood of twenty to twenty-five villagers. Enough moderates were in attendance to keep the excitable types from becoming too overwrought and forming a mob. Grimsy waited for the inevitable question. Fortunately, Mrs. Addison, a local nervous nelly, was on hand to ask it.

"We can't have those people running around. Does Chief Johns know about this?"

And there it was: Grimsy's opening. He lowered his glass and gave the other denizens of The Traveller's a penetrating stare. Firmly placing the glass on the bar with a thump like a judge's gavel, Grimsy turned and said in an ominous tone, "Chief Johns isn't back from his fishing trip up north. We're on our own."

The semi-paralyzing effect of the last three words reverberated through the patrons' thoughts. People murmured things like "fine time to go off and leave his post" and "if I'm killed in my sleep, I know who's to blame." But the most used refrain was "the police aren't what they used to be." Finally, one person sitting by herself in the warmest corner of the pub decided to slow the boil on Grimsy's pot stirring and bring a sense of ease to the uneasy.

"Merriam will be home tonight," Polly Johns, Chief Johns' mother and best promoter, said in a matter-of-fact tone. "In the meantime, let's go out and watch the boat show go by. Always did love a good canal festival."

Where there had been dread, there was now peace and a chance at outdoor entertainment. A couple of men at the bar slapped Grimsy on the back shaking their heads at his theatrics. Natural joviality returned to the crowd as they moved out to the back of the pub with their drinks. Soon enough, they saw the first boat emerge from around the bend.

If only one word was allowed to be used to describe the boats moving slowly up the canal, it would be colorful. Deep greens, bright reds and vibrant yellows enlisted the imagination of the viewer with thoughts of carnivals, exotic outsiders, and romantic mysteries.

From the bow of the first boat waved a bob, or a flag with a two-headed black eagle on a red background. Similar bobs adorned the other boats but with different items being held in the eagle's talons.

"Must be a tribe of sorts," Marvin Hathaway, the postman for Marsden-Lacey, said.

Two newly arrived patrons moseyed into the pub's back garden and gazed curiously at the three boats being tethered to the bollards, or tie-up rings, along The Traveller's mooring area.

"Hmm, Alistair," Perigrine Clark said in a reflective mood, "Interesting names on those boats, don't you think?"

Turning to Alistair, his partner, he waited for an answer. Alistair was the impeccably groomed country gentleman in his Grieves & Hawks bespoke tweed jacket, an orange collared moleskin waistcoat, wine-colored silk tie and black corded trousers. Perigrine wore a burgundy colored lambswool cardigan with check tweed trousers.

"Yes, they are. Those bobs on the boat remind me of something, too. Odd don't you think they would be flying a flag at all?"

From behind him a voice said, "No, Mr. Clark. Water travelers like other Roma people, are proud of their heritage and families almost always stay extremely close. Their flags have meaning. What is most interesting about their arrival isn't their flag but why they're here so late in the season." Chief Inspector Merriam Johns said.

Perigrine and Alistair twitched slightly at the sound of Chief Johns' voice coming up so close behind them. Their discussion about the Brontë manuscript had involved Perigrine in a dangerous game. It was important they hadn't said anything that might make the Chief suspicious of their earlier escapades.

Perigrine casually said, "You're back from Scotland, Chief? Have any luck?"

A big smile lit up Chief Johns' face. "It was exceptional fishing. Wanted to get back though. Had a feeling in my bones."

Perigrine and Alistair studied the narrowboats.

"By the way Mr. Clark and Mr. Turner," Johns continued, "I've got a job for you, if you would be interested. It's a paid job."

One of the Roma men standing on the first boat was dressed in a deep, forest green jacket emblazoned with red, blue and yellow embroidery and a bright orange scarf being used as a belt for his black parachute pants. Alistair, himself dressed somewhat vibrantly, wondered at what the Roma man must be thinking wearing such an odd assortment of colorful outerwear.

"Well, Chief, Perigrine and I are always up for making extra cash," he said with a twinkle in his eye toward Perigrine.

"I need some advice—" Johns began but he didn't get a chance to finish.

From behind him stepped his small and assertive mother, Polly Johns. She'd seen her son begin the conversation with Perigrine Clark and Alistair Turner and she knew he was about to sideline her on their current renovation project for the kitchen garden of the old stone, farm house they still shared. She expertly maneuvered herself through the crowd and intercepted his first move.

"Merriam, you know I am handling this renovation." She gave both Perigrine and Alistair a steely stare. "I've no doubt Perigrine and Alistair will give us excellent planning advice but remember this garden will be conceived as a functional garden not a foo foo flower show thing you can someday show off at one of Mrs. Addison's Garden Invitationals."

Chief Johns, a shrewd man, shrugged his shoulders and sighed quietly. Polly was bent on having a place to grow hops for her beer brewing enterprise. She typically ran the show when it came to any changes at the farm.

While they were talking, the water travelers were tying up and situating themselves in a neat row of boats along the bank. They sang a song as they went about their work. It had a melancholy feel.

By the light of the empire,
By the light of the blue hen,
By the light of the cherub,
To the grave and beyond,
To the grave and beyond.

"Rather odd song, don't you think?" Perigrine asked Alistair.

"Perhaps, but appropriate, too. It must have something to do with the names of their boats."

"Of course."

The older man, dressed in the original assortment of colorful clothes, stepped off his boat and walked up towards the Inn. His weathered, cheerful face glowed with a simple kindness and once he arrived at the top of the steps leading to the back garden, he stopped his gait, straightened himself to his full five feet five inches and cleared his throat, effectively capturing the extremely curious Marsden-Lacey public's attention.

"Hello!" he said in a voice intended to carry to even those near the back of the group. "My name is Stephan Rossar-mescro and my family and I are here to find a woman who we hope will give us answers. I would be appreciative, if someone will take me to see," he cast his eyes down to a rumpled piece of paper in his hand and finished, "Helen Ryes."

Some murmuring scuttled through the villagers. Soon all eyes turned to see if Chief Johns would be able to produce Helen from thin air. Johns' face registered nothing but his instincts told him his idea to return home early was a good one. What on Earth did these Roma people want with Helen Ryes?

Johns spoke up in a kind tone. "I'll be happy to put you in contact with her, Mr. Rossar-mescro. Why don't you come by the constabulary tomorrow morning and I'll see about setting up a meeting?"

"Thank you, Sir. I'll be there at 9:00 am. We do not want to stay this far north for long. The weather will be against us soon," Mr. Rossar-mescro said.

Alistair smiled at Perigrine and Chief Inspector Johns. "You said you had a feeling in your bones, Chief. I think it's safe to say Helen Ryes hit the top of Marsden-Lacey's most interesting people list as of ten seconds ago. What do you say to that?"

Johns didn't say anything. Instead, grabbing his jacket, he headed for Flower Pot Cottage. He needed to find Helen Ryes before anyone else did.

CHAPTER 2

Mariynsky Palace, Kiev, Russia
March 1917

THE SERVANTS OF MARIA FEODOROVNA, the Dowager Empress of Russia, were frantically packing. In a matter of days, the Bolsheviks would control Kiev. Once in the city, they would strip the palace and the Empress of her valuables and most likely imprison her. Maria, known as the Dowager Empress, mother of the former Tsar Nicholas II of the defunct Imperial Russia, worked alongside her household servants, ladies in waiting and even her faithful Cossacks to pack up the Mariynsky Palace's remaining valuables. Paintings, carpets, silver tea services, jewels and objets d'art were all being put into crates and taken to the small barge waiting in the Dnieper River below the palace. The barge would travel down the Dnieper to the Black Sea and to Ai-Todor Palace on the southern tip of the Crimea Peninsula where the remaining Imperial family was promised a certain degree of safety by the White Army from their Bolshevik pursuers.

Her world was irrevocably changed. For the last five years, storm clouds had brewed over Russia. All her pleading with her son, Nicholas, to see the disintegration of the people's support for him hadn't worked. He wouldn't heed her or his closest advisors who saw what he and Alexandra, his wife, refused to see. They chose to shut themselves away from the government, the court, the raging war with Germany, and the truth. Maria was not surprised when the people took to the streets egged on by the Bolsheviks and succeeded in deposing their Tsar, putting an end to almost a thousand years of Russia's Imperial rule. Her beloved son, Nikky, his pathetic wife and their beautiful children were imprisoned. Romanovs were being hunted down and killed, so she prayed continuously for her son's family to be spared.

Their only hope was if she successfully maneuvered enough money and valuables to a safe place so when they were freed, they would have financial security. Their many palaces in St. Petersburg, Petrograd, and Tsarskoe Selo were being looted and the valuables hauled off by the Bolshevik government to be secured in the Kremlin's Armory. Maria was trying to make haste to save at least some of her family's heritage, their memories and maybe their lives.

Those items most personal to the Dowager Empress like her jewelry, family mementos and most of her wardrobe would travel with her by train. The bulkier cargo would be put on the barge which would come down the Dnieper to the Lavidia Palace at a much slower rate. Time was critical but so many of the more fragile things needed proper handling.

It was nearly impossible to coordinate the deconstruction of a household on this massive scale. People were packing, moving items onto carts and decisions were being made without much attention to detail. Her hope was that enough things would make it to the Crimea to give all those who depended on her a chance for another life. She wouldn't leave Russia unless she had to. She would go to the southern tip of her country and cling onto its edge.

Lieutenant Ivan Ivovich, one of her Cossack body guards, entered her sitting room to update her on how the move was progressing. He stood at attention in the doorway waiting for her to speak first.

"Yes, Lieutenant?" she asked glancing up from the letter she was hurriedly writing to her sister, The Dowager Queen of England, Alexandra.

"Your Imperial Highness," he said, "we will be finished this evening. The Commander of the Red Army sends you a message."

Maria stiffened but sat perfectly still, every nerve in her body on alert.

Ivovich did something he would never do under normal conditions. He dared to look the Empress directly in the face. The severity of the situation called for him to impress upon her the importance of their immediate departure.

"The Commander remembers your charity and kindness with the people and wishes your departure to take place by tonight," he said.

It was a thoughtful attempt by the Commander to hasten Maria to a safe location.

Maria bristled. Being told what to do, being coerced, forced to flee from her home was taking its toll on her stamina and focus. They would not see her run.

Going back to the letter and holding the pen slightly above the paper, she said firmly, "I will leave in the morning. Please send the Commander an invitation to dine with me tonight. It would be my pleasure."

The woman who had been Tsarina of all of Russia, the hostess of over nine palaces, mother of six children and loving protector of the Russian people would not be dismissed from Kiev like a beggar.

The Cossack hesitated in the door. She remained steadfastly focused on the paper waiting for him to accept that she would leave on her terms.

Finally, she heard the door latch click signaling his departure and acceptance of her position. She carefully put her pen down noting that her hand didn't tremble. This pleased her.

Alone, she got up and took stock of her belongings packed, crated, and boxed for removal to the train. Everything appeared in order but she didn't see the small crate with the annual easter gifts from her husband and her son. Not comfortable with this missing crate, she told herself she would ask about it later.

The next day, the Empress Dowager of Imperial Russia, left Kiev on her private train on her own terms. She'd spent the previous evening charming the new Commander of the Red Army at dinner. The barge with her things made its way down the Dnieper River but word came from the people along the way the Bolsheviks were waiting down river to stop and impound the boat.

One of her faithful Cossacks, Ivan Ivovich Lysenko, had been left in charge of the Empress' things. Learning the boat was in immediate danger, he opened one of the smaller crates and shoved two jeweled objects down into his boots and two more into his ample coat. It was his job to see these items were well protected, and he knew to save these most favorite things of his mistress.

To avoid the soldiers waiting for the barge, he jumped the boat as it came around a bend in the river and headed south on foot towards the Yalta Peninsula in the Crimea and the Ai-Todor Palace.

Two days later, Maria made it to her lovely home and installed her family, servants and body-guards in the Ai-Todor Palace. Immediately put under house arrest, she was subject to nighttime searches of her room, removal of her personal letters and bible, and even stripped of her family photos. The boat full of her things never reached her. She stayed a prisoner in Ai-Todor for almost another year before she was finally forced to leave Russia forever.

CHAPTER 3

Flower Pot Cottage, Marsden-Lacey, England
Present Day

ALL DAY LONG THE AUTUMN wind whipped noisily around the cozy cottage belonging to Martha Littleword. Trying to wreak havoc with what was left of her flowering summer vines and naughtily rattling the window's wooden shutters, it occasionally would sneak up on the unlatched gate to the walled garden around her house and slam it with a great gust. Amos, her five-pound scraggly watch dog, would bark terrifically from the clang of the gate against the metal latch causing Martha to nearly jump out of her skin.

In between hushing Amos, cursing the wind, and periodically shuffling back and forth between her desk and the coffee pot, she tried to focus on a project she and Helen were currently involved in for a client. Martha was still wrapped in her favorite fluffy robe and on her feet she wore an oversized pair of Garfield slippers. Her wavy red hair was pinned up in a clip with a good number of wispies flying about her head.

It was her job to put the finishing touches on a spreadsheet detailing a collection for The Grange, a rare-book museum in Marsden-Lacey where she and her new best friend, Helen Ryes, recently met. Both Helen and Martha had been mixed-up in a terrifying murder investigation that nearly put a lethal end to their friendship before it even began.

Happily, they'd not only survived the ordeal but decided to work together in Helen's book conservation and restoration business. Their new partnership was only two months old, but it was proving to be a busy one which made it necessary to sometimes room together at Flower Pot Cottage while they were in Marsden-Lacey or at Helen's home in Leeds.

For the second time that afternoon, Martha was searching for her mislaid reading glasses when Amos went into another fit of barking. She scratched and growled at the front door wanting to be let out. Forgetting about the glasses, Martha went over to the door and peeked out its small half-moon window. She wasn't able to put her finger on it, and perhaps it was the wind blustering about all morning, but a weird feeling kept needling her and it was hard to shake.

Seeing the coast was clear, she opened the door and Amos bolted outside barking as viciously as five pounds would allow her to be.

"Don't you leave the garden, Amos!" Martha yelled as the furry force of nature zipped out past the gate making a beeline toward the opposite side of the street.

A horn blared and tires screamed.

Martha's heart pounded against her chest. She ran toward the garden gate, terror giving wings to her house-shoed feet.

There in the middle of the cobblestone alley, she found Chief Merriam Johns holding the tiny body of Amos.

His gaze flashed up to meet hers. Complete horror waxed across his face.

"Oh my God! Is she okay?" Martha asked the Chief of Marsden-Lacey's Constabulary.

"Come on. Get in the car. I'll get her to the veterinary clinic," Johns said as he handed the limp, white furry body to Martha. Amos was her baby and her constant companion for the last ten years. Together, they'd weathered her husband's terrible death from cancer and the departure of Kate, her daughter, for college.

Johns grabbed Martha and guided her to the other side of the police vehicle. He grabbed a blanket from the back of the car and wrapped them both. Getting in, he turned on the police vehicle's blue flashing emergency lights and headed to the other side of Marsden-Lacey and the only veterinary office in the village.

While the car moved through the tight village streets, Martha watched Amos' breathing. Blood matted the fur on her shoulder and she could tell the small dog was in pain. Tears welled up in Martha's eyes and she tenderly told Amos it was going to be okay. Johns never said a word but he would occasionally blare his siren to warn off oncoming traffic or pedestrians.

In less than five minutes, they arrived at the veterinary clinic. Martha gingerly lifted the tiny dog and hurried into the office. Johns opened the door and bellowed, "Need a doctor. Now!"

Doctor Selby bustled out of the back after hearing the commotion to see a big man dressed in a tailored brown suit and a frazzled robe-wearing red-head holding a tiny, white dog wrapped in a blanket.

"What have we got here?" he asked lifting the blanket to see the bloody shoulder. "Give her to me. I need to get her out of pain first and then we can see what damage there is."

The vet took the furry accident victim to the back. Looking around, Martha and Johns realized there were only three seats in the waiting room and these were occupied by as many people with their various pets.

No one spoke for a few minutes. Martha caught sight of her reflection in the reception window. She then stared down at her robe, strange foot attire, and reached up to poke at her tangled, messy hair. Her anger began to boil and something caught fire in her mind. She turned to Johns slowly raising her index finger, and pointed at his chest.

"You-hit-my-dog." Her finger stabbed him in his sternum with her voice growing louder. "I can't believe it. You ran over my Amos."

"Martha," Johns said backing away from her, his voice still soft and gentle. Acutely aware that everyone in the waiting room was watching him, their Chief of Police, being poked by a woman who only came up to his chin. He tried to explain what happened.

"I never saw your dog, Martha. It was an accident."

She bent her head down wearily and looked at her Garfield house slippers. With a sigh she turned around to see the other pet owners and the overweight pug return her gaze with wide-eyed stares.

In a low, menacing tone and with her finger again pointing directly at his heart, she said to Johns, "That dog better not die." But with the last word, her emotional bottom dropped out and tears again filled her eyes.

Hesitating momentarily, he cautiously approached the valentine-robe-wearing spectacle and tenderly wrapped her in his arms. At first, she was like holding a rigid piece of lumber, but slowly she melted into his embrace and allowed him to comfort her.

After about two minutes like this, the waiting room erupted into a brawl. The big-eyed pug, weighing down his human's legs, growled at the long-haired cat comfortably ensconced on a middle-aged woman's lap. The fur flew and the two owners, not without incurring some personal pain unto themselves, managed to separate the combatants. When the hoopla was at its highest pitch, Martha shyly pushed Johns away.

The man with the pug decided it was safer to stand against the farthest wall away from the still glaring, irritated cat owner. Offering Martha his seat, he lifted his hefty dog with a grunt and moved to the other side of the room flashing a nasty look at the long-haired feline being comforted by its owner with soft murmurings like "poor baby" and "that bad, bad dog."

"I don't think you'll be taking your dog home today, Mrs…?" Doctor Selby asked, coming back into the waiting room. "She's in pain and her shoulder is dislocated."

Martha, feeling a trifle awkward what with the night clothes and the public display of emotion, opened her mouth to talk but didn't get a chance to say anything. At that moment, Helen barged through the office door with a worried expression.

"I heard Amos was hit by some idiot in a swanky Volvo. Is she okay?"

Martha and Johns exchanged quick looks.

Johns cleared his throat. "That idiot would be me, I'm afraid."

Helen stopped in mid-stride toward Martha. "Sorry, Chief. That was sorely put." Turning back to Martha, she asked, "How badly was she hurt?"

Dr. Selby was still waiting for a reply, but Martha answered Helen instead. "She's in pain and they don't know enough yet. She'll need to stay. If something happens to that dog, I'll never forgive myself. Kate will be heartbroken."

Kate was Martha's daughter and was also extremely attached to Amos who lived a spoiled life when Kate was home from attending Oxford. Wrapped in blankets to protect her from the cold and fed too many treats, the furry beggar was Kate's first pet and oldest friend.

"Mrs…?" Dr. Selby interjected, "does the dog have a previous injury to her hind leg?"

Martha, quietly hoping she might get out of the vet's office without everyone knowing who she actually was, turned to the Doctor and spoke in a low voice. "Littleword. My last name is Littleword. No, Amos was never previously injured in the leg but was born with a deformity. It doesn't slow her down."

"Okay. I'd like you to come back in the morning and I'll call you this evening with what I know after we do some work on her. Please leave your number with reception."

Doctor Selby gave Martha and company a pleasant good day and excused himself.

Grinning thinly for her waiting-room audience, Martha moved toward the reception desk. “May I check on Amos before I leave?”

“Of course,” the lady wearing pink scrubs with dog bones all over them said. “Follow me. I’ll show you back.”

Once in the back, Martha gave words of encouragement through teary eyes to Amos as the veterinarian tech gave the little dog a shot for pain. Within thirty seconds she relaxed and her eyes shut.

“Is she asleep?” Martha asked hopefully.

“Yes, she’s out of pain. You can go now and we’ll call you after the Doctor has a chance to really check her out.”

With a heavy heart, Martha found Helen and Johns waiting for her in the reception room.

“Helen, would you take me home? Amos is sleeping and they’ll call me later. I don’t think I shut the front door when I ran out of the house.”

“I closed it so don’t worry. Mrs. Cuttlebirt, your neighbor, told me what happened.” Then with a mischievous smile, Helen added, “She said you left with sirens blaring and lights flashing. She was terribly excited.”

Johns turned to Helen and, changing the subject, he said, “Mrs. Ryes?”

“Chief, please call me Helen. I think we can desist with the formalities.”

“Helen,” he said again, “we've some new visitors to Marsden-Lacey today and they want to talk with you. I’ve asked for them to meet with you at the constabulary. Would you have any time in the next day or so for a meeting?”

“Sure, Chief. What time?”

"Nine o'clock work for you?"

"I'll be there."

Johns walked around to the passenger side and motioned for Martha to roll her window down. With the office hug still fresh in her mind, she gave him a sheepish smile.

"Martha, I'm sorry about Amos." His eyes flashed with emotion.

"I know it was an accident, Merriam. Thank you for everything you did."

She watched him walk over to his car. Helen got in beside her and started the engine. Turning to Martha, she studied her friend closely.

"Did I interrupt something between you and Johns?"

Martha watched Johns' Volvo slide into traffic and disappear.

"No. You didn't," she said more to herself than to Helen. "Let's go home. I think it's time for something more than tea to drink."

Helen laughed and patting Martha reassuringly on the hand, she put the car in drive and headed home.

CHAPTER 4

Kiev, Russia
April, 1917

IVAN IVOVICH LYSENKO, THE LOYAL Cossack bodyguard of the Dowager Empress Maria Feodorovna, moved quickly through Kiev alleyways trying to stay as inconspicuous as possible. He knew if he was recognized, he would be stopped and probably thrown in prison.

His family was originally from the Kuban river region in southwestern Russia. His training to be a Cossack began at birth. Tough, excellent fighters and intelligent, the Kuban Cossacks, over the last two centuries in Russia, rose up to become the fierce bodyguards of the Russian royal family. They weren't well liked by the Bolsheviks wanting to eradicate the Romanovs from Russia forever.

Lysenko's training allowed him to go for days without sleep or food. Discomfort from lack of shelter didn't bother him. With his Empress' things secreted in his overcoat, his first priority was to return them to her.

After leaving the barge, he intended to make his way south to join up with the Empress' retinue but the route was dangerous, so he had formulated another plan. He'd returned to Kiev to either hop another barge or a train heading south. It was important for him to be as inconspicuous as possible.

The Russian countryside was riddled with battling factions of White and Red Army battalions. Cossacks were seen as loyal to the Romanovs and therefore were given two choices: death or pledge their allegiance to whoever captured them. Either route was unacceptable. He was loyal to the death to his Empress.

Lysenko bartered for a change of clothes from a bargeman he met along the docks in Kiev. His shashka, or curved military saber that all Cossacks carried, hung on his belt without a scabbard. He slid it around to hang closer to his hip so it wouldn't be easily seen under his long overcoat and give him away.

The fastest way to reach the Black Sea and the Empress Dowager was to jump on one of the trains still running despite the revolution. Waiting in Kiev's busy railway station, he checked destination and arrival boards. He found a train departing for Simferopol, a city in the middle of the Crimean Peninsula but his instincts told him there would be too many chances for him to be caught if he chose this longer trip. Instead he chose the direct train heading for Odessa on the coast of the Black Sea. From there, he would get a job on a ship heading for Yalta and the Ai-Todor. The Royal party with the Empress Dowager should be there by now.

Seeing a woman with a cumbersome trunk, two bags, and a small child, he offered to carry her luggage onto the train for her. She was relieved to get the help. He saw her settled in a compartment and carried her trunk to the luggage car to the rear of the train. The porter guarding the door was a scrawny young man of about twenty. Lysenko waited patiently until all the other passengers storing luggage departed. He approached the porter carrying the trunk easily in both his arms. The young man regarded the trunk and gave a sigh.

"I'll put it in the car," Lysenko offered.

Since the revolution began, families were fleeing south and cramming as much of their belongings as possible into their luggage, and having one less heavy trunk to lift put a smile on the porter's face.

Stepping aside, he watched Lysenko put the trunk down. With a swiftness ingrained from years of military training, Lysenko whipped around and dealt the young porter a well-executed punch to the back of his head. The boy-man never saw it coming and crumpled to the floor, unconscious.

Lysenko quickly stripped the man of his porter jacket and hat. He carried him to the rear of the car as far away from the door as possible. Binding the man's arms and legs, Lysenko also gagged him.

Like a rolled carpet, Lysenko surrounded him with various bags and trunks to hide him from view. Taking the keys out of the porter's pocket, he locked the door from the inside. Lysenko made himself comfortable, and ate the delicious baked bun filled with cabbage, or a piroshki, he bought in the market earlier. If and when someone came to the back for something, he would pretend to be the porter. Only the other train staff would think it odd, but he would say the first porter became ill and he was his replacement.

Two days passed uneventfully. When the porter woke up, he grumbled but Lysenko threatened to hit him again. Handing him food and water, he got the young man quieted down. Once they reached Odessa, Lysenko left the train with the door ajar to the luggage car. The first passengers trying to collect their things would find the young porter and free him.

The Odessa waterfront named Primorsky (Seaside) Boulevard, ran above the port of Odessa. Shaded by acacia trees first imported from Vienna in the eighteenth century, the lovely, old boulevard overlooked the Black Sea. The weather was cool but the southern seaside landscape brought to mind happy days he'd spent with the royal family during their stays here.

Shaking off thoughts of the past, Lysenko made his way to the ships tied up at the waterfront hoping to find passage to the Crimean Peninsula.

There talking with other sailors, he found a boat leaving that evening. The voyage would take about four days and would end at Sevastopol, the main port on the Crimea. From there, he would go overland to Yalta and the Ai-Todor Palace.

One of the sailors he spoke with along the docks said he'd heard the Tsar was under house arrest in Tsarskoe Selo and that the Empress was also under house arrest in the Crimea. A brigade of sailors kept her prisoner and no one was allowed in or out.

Lysenko understood then that it was impossible to ever reach the Dowager Empress again. There would be no way to get to the Ai-Todor Palace now. His long military experience served him best in moments like this. Another man less accustomed to the vicissitudes of war could be slowed or crushed by news so grim, but not Lysenko. He stayed focused.

There was only one way to return the valuables hidden in his coat. He would have to get to London or Denmark. In London, he would return the objects to her sister, the Dowager Queen Alexandra of Britain, or if he made it to Denmark and Hvidøre, Maria's private home near Copenhagen, he would be able to see her brother, the King.

He made up his mind. There were fabulous sailing ships from almost every country in the world heading to the Mediterranean. The war made his choice easy as to what kind of ship he should work on: a Spanish one. Spain's neutrality allowed her ships to sail unencumbered by constant stops and searches. It took a month of delicate enquiries but by the end of May he left Odessa on a boat carrying grain to Barcelona. If he was lucky and found other ships to work on along the way, he would be in London in half a year.

On May 23, 1917, Ivan Ivovich Lysenko, a Kuban Cossack whose family called the Kuban their home for over seven hundred years, sailed away from the docks of Odessa. He locked his gaze on the retreating Russian landscape. Something deep inside told him he might never see his homeland again. "Cossacks don't cry" he remembered his mother telling him as a child. So, he stood instead on the stern of a foreign ship, and in the military stance of his Cossack heritage, gripped the shashka's handle and paid homage to his beloved home as it slipped forever out of sight.

CHAPTER 5

Marsden-Lacey Constabulary
Present Day

ARRIVING AT THE VILLAGE CONSTABULARY the following morning, Helen's attire was professional and elegant. She wore a black, knee-length shirt dress and a lovely Burberry fawn-colored trench coat. With a nod to the crisp autumn weather, she had tied a cranberry, knit scarf loosely at her neck and completed the look with black leather knee boots and matching tights. Her dark auburn hair was cropped in a wispy, short style and as she shut her car door, she realized she'd forgotten to grab the right shoulder bag with her laptop. Only one thing to do: see if Martha would drop it by the constabulary on her way over to Healy House, the home of Piers Cousins, where they'd be meeting later.

As she dialed the number on her phone, she thought about Piers. Their trip to Florida to see her ex-husband, George, and his young fiancé, Fiona's wedding ceremony went well considering the awkwardness of watching the man she thought she would be married to for the rest of her life swapping forever oaths with a woman only slightly older than George and Helen's daughter, Christine.

Piers' presence gave her a sense of having an ally, someone there and exclusively in her corner. It was comforting, but her skittishness when it came to trust issues, made her keep a barrier up between them even though she found him extremely attractive.

Piers was attentive, fun and charming during the entire four days in Orlando where the wedding took place. She hadn't invited him to go with her to Florida, but he made up some excuse about friends in Key West that he wanted to see which he never visited even once. Nevertheless, she kept the handsome man at bay during the Orlando extravaganza mainly because she was confused about her own feelings.

As she stood in front of the Marsden-Lacey Constabulary digging in her purse for her phone, she wondered at her own reticence regarding Piers. He was on the edge of being too good to be true and it rattled her confidence. Dark-haired, tall, wealthy and kind, he was a catch. The only problem was how other women seemed to want to catch him, too.

She heard the phone begin to ring and finally found it buried under her wallet.

"Hey, what's up?" Martha asked on the other end, sounding much more cheerful than she'd been when Helen left earlier that morning.

"You sound like you got some good news."

"I did. Amos is up and better this morning. Can't pick her up until this afternoon so I'm heading for Healy."

Helen was walking toward the front door of the constabulary.

"Would you bring my laptop to me? I left it at the house this morning. Probably by the sofa."

"You bet. I'll be there in five minutes."

"Thanks, Martha," she said and put the phone away.

Reaching the door, Helen swung it open and saw Donna, one of the Marsden-Lacey constables, sitting at the reception desk and talking on the phone. They exchanged friendly waves and Helen sat down on one of the chairs. Somewhere in the back, she heard Chief Johns laughing with another man. The voices crescendoed as they came closer to the reception area. Johns emerged from the passageway and she saw he was with a small, dark-haired man of about fifty dressed in warm clothing, the kind one would wear if working out in the cold all day. They walked up to where she was sitting and she rose to meet them.

"Mr. Rossar-mescro, this is Mrs. Helen Ryes, the lady you wished to speak with."

The man's weathered face broke into a shy smile and he offered his hand which she took feeling its roughness and accepting his firm shake.

"A pleasure to meet you, Mrs. Ryes. We've come a long way to see you. Time is not on our side and we hope you can give us your help."

Helen was completely taken with the small, wiry man's demeanor. There was a timelessness surrounding him. Baffled by her own disoriented feeling, she shook the impression off and said, "I have the feeling, Mr. Rossar-mescro, the pleasure is all mine."

"If you'll both follow me, we can talk in the conference room," Johns said.

They made their way down the hall. Once they sat down, Mr. Rossar-mescro reached inside his down coat to a pocket within and pulled out a folded document. He carefully opened it. The paper was creased and showed signs of age. Excitement tingled in Helen's chest, a sensation she experienced whenever she was near a book or document dripping with significance. She stifled her desire to see it only handled with gloves. It was like nails on a chalkboard for her when she watched things not being cared for correctly.

The man handed her the document and Helen studied it for a moment. It was a letter with four short lines written underneath.

"Mr. Rossar-mescro where did you find this?" Helen asked.

The man shook his head and laughed in a puzzled tone. "It was a strange thing. My Baba Sophia pointed it out to us when we were doing work on one of the sleeping cabins in my sister's boat. As we pulled out the bed to replace the wall behind it, and we found this paper tucked into a leather pouch fixed to the bed's wooden base."

"Mr. Rossar-mescro, this document is in Russian. Did you want it translated or do you want it to go through a conservation process to have it stabilized?"

He replied simply, "I want to know what it says."

Helen didn't want to let him down. "I'm sorry, Sir, but you need a person able to translate Russian."

Mr. Rossar-mescro's expression showed his confusion. "Ms. Ryes, the woman in Nottingham said you were a specialist."

Helen's eyebrows furrowed slightly. She hated disappointing him. "The woman in Nottingham? What was her name?"

"I didn't know her. My daughter, Laura met with her."

"Did she know me or did we work together in the past?" Helen dug deeper.

"Laura told her about the recent find of this letter and how we didn't know if it was valuable. She took it for awhile and returned one evening saying she knew of a woman in Marsden-Lacey who might be able to help us. She pressed it back on Laura."

Helen considered the letter for a few moments. An uneasiness came upon her, like something or someone was whispering to her. It was unnatural and uncomfortable.

"Sir, I do happen to know a man who is a translator. His name is Thomas Albright and he is a retired military colonel. He used to work for the Government Communications Headquarters but now lives in a small village outside Nottingham. If you would like, I'll copy this document and show it to him. It might take him some time, but he may be the most qualified person to translate it for you."

A bright smile broke out across the weathered face. "Thank you Ms. Ryes. I will leave it with you. You take it to your Colonel. Show him. We'll wait here in Marsden-Lacey for another week. Our home waters are in the south on the River Wey and we want to be there soon."

Helen smiled. Something about this kind, gentle man made her want to help. "I'll see to it today, Mr. Rossar-mescro. It might take some time though."

He waved his hands as if to shoo away a tiresome worry. "Do not fret about us, dear lady. We are fine. Plenty of food, plenty of laughter. We are patient people. We can wait." With a sudden bright expression, he said, "You come to dinner tonight to our camp. Bring your man. We'll play our songs and eat together." He ended his invitation by picking up her hand and lightly kissing it on the top.

Helen blushed and smiled. It would be a cold female soul not charmed by such an old-world gesture. "I would love to come. What time should we be there?"

"We like to begin as the sun starts to set. Please be welcome." Turning to Chief Johns, he gave a short nod and said, "You come, too."

Johns' eyes flashed with curiosity. "I'll be there. You've piqued my interest."

Helen thought of something. "Mr. Rossar-mescro, what are the names of your boats?"

He smiled and said, "The Empire, the Cherub, and the Blue Hen. My Baba Sophia named them almost a hundred years ago."

Johns piped up, "Those names were in the song you were singing yesterday."

"Yes, Baba always sang the song and we've passed it down over the years."

Helen paused at Stephan's last comment. "I thought you said your Baba Sophia pointed this letter out to you when you were doing some recent work on your sister's boat?"

"I did say that."

"She must be well over one hundred years old then, if she named the boats so long ago."

"No," Stephan said simply, "she is dead. My Baba Sophia is a ghost. She's always with us keeping a watch over the boats and her family."

Johns and Helen exchanged quick glances and didn't press Stephan further.

Mr. Rossar-mescro got up to leave. He tipped his hat to Helen and the Chief and turned to go.

"Bring your friends. We Romani know good people. Any friend of yours is a friend of ours."

He waved to them from the office door and as Helen and Johns watched, Mr. Rossar-mescro walk briskly down the hall and he was gone.

CHAPTER 6

The Port of Dover England
November 1917

THE BURLEY RUSSIAN MAN'S BREATHING was raspy and the terrible fever raging in his body was tenaciously beginning to take its toll on his will to fight the illness. A petite, dark-haired young woman worked tirelessly trying to spoon-feed him water.

Ivan's suffering was shared by ten other hard-working souls on the Spanish grain freighter. Already eight had died from the flu. Their ship made port in Dover the previous night and the British authorities put the boat and its crew in quarantine. No one was allowed to leave or come on the ship. The crew's only option was to wait for death to finish his job and pass from their midst and on to other fertile pastures.

Sophia Argintari, the young woman so dedicated to watching over the Russian man, was only seventeen. One of many dispossessed people from the ongoing World War, she had lost her mother and sister recently during the German siege of Constanta, a port in Romania on the Black Sea. Sophia alone survived.

The days following the assault on Constanta had been horrific. At first, she didn't have the will to leave her mother's and younger sister's bodies still lying in the rubble of the small house they'd lived in. No one came to help. Many of her people were killed because the quarter they called home was poorly built.

Two days after the shelling was done and triumphant German troops marched through the streets, Sophia went to find a priest. She needed to have her mother's and sister's bodies blessed and hopefully buried.

Because so many people had died during the shelling, the priest promised he would try to be there in a few days time. He gave her holy water to sprinkle over the bodies as a blessing and a pail of lime to cover them with to inhibit the smell of decomposition.

After two more days, those left alive in her Romani community came out to find each other. They took their dead on carts to be buried in mass graves dug by the city officials. There to mark their grave, Sophia wrote both her mother's name, Mavia, and her sister's, Sasha, on a white stone. She pledged to one day find a way to give them a more decent memorial.

Her family in Constanta was gone but her Romani family was still strong throughout other European countries. Sophia packed a small bag, dressed herself as a man and went down to the sun-drenched port where the ships still arrived for their intended cargo of either grain or oil.

A Spanish ship offered her work. The captain appraised her with his eyes as if to decide if a young boy was up to the demand of work on a freighter, but in the end she more than pulled her weight. They gave her work in the galley and before they'd reached Sicily, she was delighting the crew with delicious recipes from her native homeland such as mamaliga, a traditional cornbread, or a vegetable ghivetch served with fried pastries and filled with meat or sometimes with fruit.

It was the big thoughtful Russian named Ivan who appreciated Sophia's food the most. It reminded him of his mother's cooking from when he was a boy. She guessed he was probably aware of her true sex, but kept her secret, and when possible, he offered to help carry the heavier work load for her. They became friends, two refugees brought together by a common appreciation for food and the loss of the same home.

A malaise settled on the crew after leaving the port of Barcelona. Starting with a fever it progressed to vomiting or coughing and chills. Three of the stricken men were showing signs of getting better but not Ivan.

He signaled for Sophia to help him sit up. Because of his illness, they moved him to a small storage room where a pallet was made on the floor for him to lie on. The small room had one amenity: a porthole that opened. Fresh air from the sea meandered into the cramped squalid metal hole made by men. It softly nourished the room with a sense of tranquility and reminded him with gentle whispers breathed across his fevered skin of the wide-open stretches of land where the wind roamed freely in the Kuban.

Sophia propped him up and waited for him to gather the strength to speak. He opened his eyelids with effort to reveal blood-shot eyes surrounded by dark, sunken flesh.

"In the corner is a satchel," he whispered.

She easily reached for it in the cramped room and laid it next to him so it touched his hand.

"Inside," he said.

Carefully she unlaced the leather ties and pulled the flap back. There were four bundled objects wrapped in linen. Down beneath these was a glint of something shiny.

"Do you want me to take these things out?" she asked.

Shaking his head no, he said, "There is a letter. I need you to take these things to the Queen…"

His voice faltered and his breathing became quick. He shut his eyes and she watched as he took one, two deep breaths trying to calm himself. With his eyes shut, he quietly said, "I need to trust you to take these things to Her Majesty The Queen of England. The sister of my Empress, Maria Feodorovna."

Sophia at first thought he was delusional from his fever. For a long moment she stared at the ravaged face of the man brought so low by his fight with the illness. His eyes were shut and from his breathing she knew he was sleeping from the exertion of trying to speak.

Reaching inside the satchel, she pulled one of the linen-wrapped items out, feeling its heaviness. Carefully she unwound the fabric strips and with a short intake of air, she beheld a thing so exquisitely wrought, it was as if God himself had his hand upon its design.

Up against the inside wall of the satchel was a piece of paper neatly folded. She took it out and studied it. Recognizing it must be written in Russian, she wasn't able to read it.

"Sophia," Ivan struggled to talk as his hand pointed to a short list within the body of the letter. "Each one has a name: Empire, cherub, mauve and blue hen," he read to her. "These are what they are called. Don't forget."

For a long while she sat by the dying man wondering at the hand fate was dealing her. She put the bag with the beautiful bejeweled things back in the corner she'd pulled it from.

Ivan's breath was slowing and he moaned in his sleep. Sophia, wearied from the sleepless nights and the long journey she had endured, took the bear-paw of a hand and held it. Tears formed in her tired eyes and rolled down her small face. One more death made her think back on her mother and sister.

The air in his chest rattled and he convulsed once, twice and he moved no more. A soft gust of sea air pushed its way through the porthole into the tiny room. She watched as it swirled around, lightly moving the hair on the man's damp head. With a gentle caress, the wind tried to release the imprisoned soul within. And as if the body no more held power over the spirit to hold it, one finale exhalation of breath let Ivan escape the confines of his flesh and ride the air out through the small porthole and homeward forever.

CHAPTER 7

Healy House
Present Day

HELEN AND MARTHA DECIDED TO ride together from the constabulary to Healy House, Piers Cousins' lovely Elizabethan estate outside Marsden-Lacey.

The day was turning chilly and the glory of the changing autumn colors along the countryside lanes and rolling pastures, made for an uplifting and scenic trip to Healy. As they drove along, Martha worked on the laptop going over a spreadsheet. The girls were two months into a conservation project for Piers' library. They'd finished compiling an inventory and were creating a detailed condition report for each book in need of conservation.

"Thanks for bringing my laptop earlier. You missed meeting an interesting fellow though. He was the water traveler from the narrowboats that arrived yesterday," Helen said as she maneuvered the car through the twisting, hedge-bordered rural lane.

"What was he like? I've always wanted to be a water traveler. Someday we should rent a narrowboat and take a holiday. We'd see so many beautiful byways of England. What do ya say? Doesn't the idea of meandering around the countryside stopping at every small village, tasting its food offerings and lolling around in cozy pubs, sound wonderful? We should stop and check out some of the Romani's boats."

"I'm not sure it's as romantic a notion as you think it is. If Mr. Rossar-mescro's hands are any indication of the work level it requires to be a boat handler, I'm probably not made of the right stuff."

"Ah, his hands are probably rough from being a carpenter or something. Everything I've read on narrowboat holidays says it's simple. Even a child is able to handle the steering. Besides, we could go with some friends and share the work load." Martha mused for a moment. "Probably need to take Amos, Gus and Vera though."

Helen shook her head and narrowed her eyes though still focusing on the road ahead. The thought of taking two cats, one dog, Martha, God knows how many of Martha's friends, and a mountain of luggage, all on a small, cramped narrowboat made her decide to change the subject quickly.

"It was the oddest feeling I got from meeting him. Like someone else was in the room but not at the same time."

"What do you mean? Like a ghost?" Martha asked.

"Well, it was more like the document he showed me was weighted with history. Do you know what I mean?" Helen said.

"Sounds like the document was haunted."

"Haunted" expressed the feeling exactly. It had been an odd experience. She decided to change the subject again to something lighter.

"So, I'm going to a real Roma dinner tonight," she said brightly.

"Me, too," Martha chimed in.

"The Chief?"

"Yep."

Helen gave Martha an affectionate pat on the arm. "You two are cute together."

"He's been so thoughtful after nearly killing my dog."

Helen burst out laughing.

"What?" Martha asked as if taken aback and added, "He *has* been thoughtful."

"It's the way you say things."

"Well, he did nearly kill my dog. But to his credit, he is trying to do the right thing."

Finally arriving at Healy, Helen stopped the car in front of the old manor home. Healy inspired in her visitors a delicious sense of anticipation for what the interior might hold. Mullioned windows and vine covered ancient oak timbers grounded the sprawling house neatly in the middle of the sixteenth century. At this time of year only a few flowers graced her front with hints of summer memories.

The girls hadn't been to Healy in nearly a month. Their busy schedule had kept their communication with Piers Cousins to phone calls and emails. In that time, Piers had received custody of his new ward, Emerson Carstons.

Helen wondered how Piers was managing his new parental duties. He'd been given complete charge of Emerson by the child's legal family due to the fact that both of Emerson's parents were dead and no one else was able to take the child to raise. All of this was perfectly fine with Piers, who had believed for years that Emerson was his son and worked tirelessly to have custody of him.

Martha flung her purse over her shoulder and slammed her car door. “Has Piers found a housekeeper yet? Hope he does a better job of hiring the next one. Might want to suggest a psychological screening during the selection process as a precaution against crazies.”

Helen rolled her eyes heavenward searching for an answer. She followed Martha up the steps to the front door feeling nervous butterflies fluttering in her stomach. She hadn’t seen Piers in over a month and the thought of seeing him was a heady mixture of excitement and awkwardness. They pulled the bell chain and, while waiting for the door to be opened, turned around to take in the view of the front lawn which gently sloped down to the river Calder far below in the distance.

The door opened and there standing in the entrance was a lovely young woman wearing a simple cream colored blouse with a peter-pan collar and a light blue button-up cardigan. She wore a brown tweed skirt hitting right above her knee and at her throat hung a simple strand of pearls. Her long blonde hair was pulled up into a loose chiffon bun at the base of her neck. She needed no make-up to highlight her already lovely skin.

Helen was awestruck by the prettiness of the younger woman as she introduced herself.

“Hello, I’m Celine Rupert. I’m the new housekeeper and nanny. Mr. Cousins is expecting you,” she said with a warm smile. “Please come in and I’ll show you to the library.”

The girls exchanged “Wow!” expressions once Celine’s back was safely turned to them. They followed her into the house’s interior. Helen guessed her to be no more than thirty and the woman's accent implied she was from the upper classes if not the English gentry.

"So how do you like working for *old* Piers?" Martha asked.

Celine's back didn't tense at Martha's familiarity nor did she slow her pace toward the library. "Mr. Cousins is an excellent employer, as I'm sure you know."

Martha winked at Helen and mouthed the word "feisty."

Helen mouthed the words "shut up" back at Martha.

They reached the door of the library and Celine knocked firmly.

"Come in!" Piers called from the inside.

Opening the door for them, Celine followed them inside and said, "Mr. Cousins, the ladies you were expecting."

"Thank you, Celine. That will be all."

For a brief moment after her departure Helen, Martha and Piers were mute. There was a smidgen of awkwardness in the room with so many unsaid thoughts.

Piers jumped in where angels feared to tread. "So, that's Celine. A wonderful girl. Absolutely amazing nanny. She's been with Emerson since he was born. Loves him like a mother."

Martha and Helen blinked and it was Helen who, in a crisp, professional tone said, "She's a lovely woman, Piers, and I'm glad things are working out for you. Do we get to meet Emerson today?"

Piers' face brightened with joy. "Of course! I can't wait for you to meet him. He'll be home from school about three o'clock. We could have tea together."

"That would be perfect. Martha and I have some more work to do until then," Helen said.

"Great idea. I'll meet you back here around two-thirty. We can go over your suggestions. I've got some things to see about until then."

Martha and Helen went on with their work until the mantel clock chimed two times letting them know it was time for Piers to return. The library door's familiar squeak of the hinges caught their attention.

"Are you at a stopping point?" Piers asked entering the room.

"Perfect timing. I'm dying for a cup of tea," Martha said sitting down in one of the wingback chairs by the fireplace.

"Celine is on her way with the tea cart."

Martha's phone began to ring. "I'd better take this. If you'll both excuse me."

They watched Martha let herself out of the room.

"I'm so pleased you came by today," Piers said once they were alone. "I've missed you."

Helen smiled kindly back at Piers and laying her hand on his she replied in a friendly, up-beat way, "I've missed you, too, and I'm excited to see Emerson. Is it going well?"

Piers shook his head in bemusement. "He's such a bright boy and so full of life, Helen. He's attached to Celine and happy with this as his home. It's a lot to ask of a child but he understands I'm not his father. I've made it my number one mission in life to be a father to him, if not his real one."

The door to the library creaked open and Martha stuck her head in.

"Guess who I found peeking at me through the balusters of the stairs?" she asked.

With a big smile on her face, she pushed the door further open and walked in holding the hand of a small, blonde boy.

Piers stood up and with a big grin on his face, motioned for the boy to come forward. "Emerson, come here. I want to introduce you to two of my dear friends."

Still holding Martha's hand and shyly studying Helen, Emerson walked toward them. He stood a few inches over four feet tall and was solid in build. His hair was thick and slightly wavy and was trimmed in a typical school-boy short style. Two dimples could be seen when he smiled and two skinned knees hinted at the typical happy play of a young boy.

"Mrs. Ryes and Mrs. Littleword, I would like to introduce Emerson Carstons," Piers said with no small hint of pride in his voice.

Emerson was well versed in meeting older people and Celine's skills in preparing her young ward were obvious. He offered his hand to both Helen and Martha saying, "Good afternoon, Madam. It's a pleasure to meet you."

Celine stood quietly at the door waiting to collect Emerson. Piers saw her standing there and said, "I would like Emerson to take tea with us this afternoon. Would you like to join us Celine?"

"Mr. Cousins, Senior Agosto wants help with the grocer's delivery. I think I'd better not keep him waiting," she said.

"Yes, of course. Thank you," Piers replied.

After Celine departed, the three adults spent a lively half-hour swapping stories with Emerson about his school day and remembrances of their own from many years ago. His skinned knees were from an afternoon of playing pole-switch, a game highly enjoyed by all first and second grade children according to him.

After tea was finished, Piers gave the boy a biscuit, or cookie, to hide in his pocket for a later treat saying, "Well, off you go, Emerson. I'll be up later and we can use the old telescope to see how Mr. Chattersworth is getting along with his fox trap down by the river."

Wearing a huge grin for Piers, Emerson nodded and said, "Thank you." He turned to Helen and Martha and said, "Goodbye. It was a pleasure to meet you."

They watched the child walk to the door. With a soft click of the latch, he was gone.

Martha turned to Piers. "He's adorable. It goes fast, enjoy every minute. I'm still in shock Kate's in college."

As she finished, her phone rang again. The name flashing was "Fuzzy."

"I've got to take this. Excuse me." Martha walked out of the room leaving Helen and Piers to return to their own conversation.

"Martha is right. Emerson is a sweet, beautiful child and Celine is doing a wonderful job. He's been fortunate to have you both in his life." Helen paused, remembering the

Roma dinner that evening. “Would you want to go to a truly unique dinner under the stars tonight?”

Piers flashed his blue eyes and smiled. “Are you asking me out, Mrs. Ryes?”

Helen never hesitated. “I am. Want to go?”

“Are you picking me up?” Piers asked.

“No,” she said flatly, “but how about I meet you on Barbel Bridge at sundown. We can go together from there. Bring a bottle of wine. I’ll bring the cups.”

A mischievous grin played at the corner of Piers’ mouth. “I’ll be there. Sounds romantic.”

Martha swung back into the room triumphantly.

Helen finished up the invitation with Piers by saying, “Okay, I’ll see you there. I think Martha and I should get going.”

Martha collected the laptop and her purse while also texting someone on her phone. As she stuffed these items into a dark leather satchel, she said, “Thank you, Piers, for the tea and it was so nice to meet Emerson. By the way, Celine, is probably too young for you.”

“Martha!” Helen exclaimed, completely shocked by Martha’s announcement.

“What?” Martha asked. “He’s too old for her.” She went back to putting things in the bag. “I’m only saying that because I like him and he needs to consider his own welfare.”

Both Piers and Helen shared an expression of perplexed amusement on their faces. Piers stood up and going over to Martha, he turned her around by the shoulders to face him.

Martha smiled up at him with an eyebrow arched for effect. "Y-e-s?"

Piers gave her a squeeze. "Thank you, Martha."

She gave him a motherly pat on his shoulder. "I want to see you with someone who might really care for you, Piers. That's all."

"I know."

"Well, if we're all done here with the touchy-feely stuff, I've got to get home and decide what one wears to a Roma shindig," Martha said as she headed for the door with Helen following behind her.

"Roma…shindig?" Piers asked.

"You heard the woman. See you on the Barbel Bridge and don't be late," Helen cheerfully replied. Turning one last time, she gave him a winning wink and pulled the library door closed behind her.

CHAPTER 8

London, England
March 1918

FOR THE LAST THREE MONTHS Sophia Argintari had been living and working in a small inn near Billingsgate Fish Market along the Thames in London. A rough and rowdy crowd called Billingsgate home, but liking the humor and warmth of the English people, Sophia decided to stay there while she searched for her family she knew were in England.

After the ship's quarantine was lifted the previous December, she asked one of the sailors if they knew of a place in London where she might stay cheaply. The Turbot Inn was well liked by the barge men and sailors. The food was simple, good and a fair price while the portly publican and his wife were honest, kind people who gave her a room near the kitchen to call her own. In return she did the cooking and the kitchen housekeeping for a small wage.

Sophia's favorite activity was to go down to one of the many wharfs along the Thames to try to find other Romani people who might know of her own family living in England. She'd kept the beautiful, jewel-encrusted things and the long gold-handled saber her friend the Russian gave her before he died. She knew their value was beyond her understanding. It terrified her thinking someone would find them in her belongings and think she'd stolen them.

No one would ever believe a poor Roma girl's story and would immediately take her to the authorities.

For the last three months while living in London, Sophia kept the valuable things wrapped and hidden behind a piece of wood floor trim in the wall of her bedroom. Things that once graced the gilded rooms of the wealthiest royals in European history and were considered to have cost millions of dollars when they were first made by gifted artisans, were wrapped in pieces of dirty linen and stuffed in a dark hole where only mice and spiders crawled indifferently by.

She never dared to approach the large palace where she knew the British Royal family lived in London. Many times she'd gone to stare through the bars but her nerve failed her whenever the soldiers with the tall, fluffy black hats marched by. What if they put her in jail or worse, killed her, because they thought she'd stolen the jeweled things? She would wait until she found someone she really trusted to tell her story to. Until then what she had hidden in the plaster wall of a tired kitchen pub would stay put.

Sophia's first spring in London was full of new sights and sounds. Though the specter of the first world war still brutalized almost every corner of Europe, the dark clouds were breaking up for Sophia. She learned from other Romani people working on the docks and wharfs nearby, of a possible relative living on a canal boat near Weybridge, a town only a short ride south of London.

She was told they were bargee, or barge people, who carried cargo such as coal, timber or wheat on their barges up and down the rivers and canals to either warehouses, granaries or mills. The bargee also lived on their boats with their family. Sophia's chances of finding her relative were good because the name Argintari was unique among the Romani people.

On one of her days off, she decided to go down to Billingsgate Fish Market. There was a Roma fishwife, Mrs. Rossar-mescro, who ran a herring stall. The Turbot Inn, where Sophia cooked, bought herring from Mrs. Rossar-mescro every Tuesday. So, since the inn was a good customer, Sophia was safe in asking a small favor of the fishwife.

The still cold March wind cut through her thin coat and laughed at the wretched state of Sophia's stockings as she walked down the tight alleyways leading to the market. That morning Sophia asked for her wages and stopped along the way at the tobacconists. Mrs. Rossar-mescro would enjoy some tobacco to use in her pipe. A treat, no matter how small, would be much appreciated by any of the rough and tough fishwives of Billingsgate.

Once inside, the wind lost its power among the throng of humanity, carts and stalls. Sophia looked for the herring stalls, but before she saw Mrs. Rossar-mescro, she heard her. Loud, pushy and foul-mouthed, the solidly built dark-haired woman kept her hawking banter going while she wrapped fish, haggled with customers and took money.

"Good morning, Mrs. Rossar-mescro," Sophia said as soon as it was her turn to talk with the hard-selling matron. "I've got something to ask of you."

"What is it, lass? Be quick about it. I'm about business you know."

"I need to find my family near Weybridge. Who would I ask to take me that far? Someone you would trust."

Not missing a beat, Mrs. Rossar-mescro took money from a tall, shabbily dressed restaurant porter, wrapped six fish in waxy paper and answered Sophia. "My son, Barty. He'll take you. Leaves for that direction each morning. Got to be here by six o'clock in the morning. Meet me here. He comes by for his meal."

Sophia pulled out the small paper bag neatly folded by the boy in the tobacco store and handed it to the strong, gruff talking woman of about forty years of age.

"Here, Mrs. Rossar-mescro. Thank you. I will be here next Tuesday to go with him."

The older woman's eyebrows raised at the girl's good business acumen. Giving a small, yet thoughtful gift, especially when money was so precious, spoke volumes among people who understood the value of a penny. Mrs. Rossar-mescro knew Sophia was miserably poor but the young girl wasn't asking for something for nothing. The woman opened the small bag and took a sniff.

"Thank you, lass," she said with a tender smile. "I'll be seeing you Tuesday."

Sophia thanked her and hurried away, letting Mrs. Rossar-mescro get back to what put food on the table. Later, after a small minced pie she bought in the market, Sophia went down to the docks and sent a message with another bargee man who claimed to know her family. She gave him two pence to deliver a note telling them she would be coming next Tuesday and hoped to meet them. He promised to deliver the note and to tell them of her. Sophia must wait and hope that they would be interested in her.

The following week took forever for a young girl eager to find her family. When Tuesday came, it found Sophia racing down the back streets in the early hours of the chilly morning toward the fish market and Mrs. Rossar-mescro's stall. There standing by the stall was a young man so pretty that Sophia nearly stumbled once she locked her gaze on him. She slowed her quick pace to a hesitant walk, nervous to know if this was the Barty she was supposed to travel to Weybridge with this morning.

With a deep breath, Sophia calmed herself and approached the stall.

"Ah, there you are my dear. Get on with you both. Barty will take you to Weybridge and bring you home." Mrs. Rossar-mescro turned to Barty. "I'll expect you to bring me some news from your Baba. She's with your Bebee Marie. They'll feed you both."

Mrs. Rossar-mescro returned to calling in her loud sing-song voice about her herrings indicating to both Sophia and Barty it was time to move along and not encumber possible customers approaching the stall.

The young man motioned for Sophia to follow him. His extreme shyness kept him from meeting her eyes when she asked him how far it was to the boat. It began to rain as they made it down to the lower docks below the fish market where barges, skiffs and punts were tied along the wharf. Strong men, boys and even women were busy unloading all kind of fish known to England's waters whether it be sea or river. Barty maneuvered around carts and basket-toting people, guiding Sophia to a long watercraft tied up at the end of the dock. It was known as a sailing barge, an extremely versatile and economical vessel for carrying cargo along the Thames and her estuaries.

The rain came down in a light drizzle as the two young people stepped onto the barge and Barty untied the ropes holding it secure to the dock. Sophia lent a hand, and for doing so, received a quick nod and a smile from the still reticent, dark-eyed young man. A Thames barge only needed a small sail to maneuver it up the river. The wind was high today from the early morning storm, so once the sail took the wind, the barge moved with ease and spirit toward its destination.

"Do you know your family you are going to see?" Barty asked as he stood at the wheel steering the barge.

"No, I've never met them. I know of them. It's my father's family."

"Are you going to live with them, if they take you?"

"Yes, I miss my family," Sophia said in a small voice.

Barty couldn't have known that his question touched on her deepest fear. What if they wouldn't take her? What if they weren't her family? What if they didn't get her message and they weren't even there? It had been almost a year since she lost her mother and sister. Her life was about survival, fear and loneliness. Sophia held on to the small crucifix necklace she wore, rubbing it and praying she would find the love she'd lost.

In two hours the barge reached the town of Weybridge and Barty easily docked the boat near a busy place. Sophia helped him wrap the lines securely around the bollards and followed him to where many other barges were tethered along the banks. It didn't take long for Barty to find his own clan and, with Sophia in tow, he took her to meet the matriarch of the family, Baba Nadya, Barty's grandmother.

Immediately, the small woman with her grey hair tied up with two bright blue scarves, took Sophia by the shoulders and stared into the girl's eyes reading the sad story there. Nothing was said for a few moments. The mother of five and grandmother of more than twenty, pulled the young girl to her breast and hugged her for a long time cooing and murmuring words women and children recognize instinctually as sounds of comfort. Something cracked and burst inside the young Romanian girl's heart. For a few long minutes, she simply cried in the safe arms of a woman who nurtured her soul and understood her tragedy.

Sophia soon sat up and hugged the Baba and, giving her a shy smile, she leaned in and kissed the wizened woman's soft cheek.

"The ones you search for are not here, small one," Baba Nadya said. "Barty will take you along the dock and the banks but you will not find them. God has sent you to us. If you wish to stay among the Rossar-mescros, we'll claim you as our own. Go child and try to find your people, but come home to your family when you are ready."

For the next four hours, Sophia and Barty talked with every boatman, bargee family and dock worker along the Wey River where it meets the Thames. The family Argintari no longer called the Wey and the Thames their home. They'd gone north to work the coal barges near Sheffield.

As the sun settled in the afternoon sky, it was time to leave and make their way back to London. This time as they boarded the barge, Barty made haste to step onto the boat first. He turned to face Sophia who stood close to the edge of the dock perplexed at his sudden hurry. Barty held out both hands to help her make the jump. Her smile showed how hesitant she was, but she took his hands and made the leap. They shared a brief, but weighted gaze for one another. In less than a month, Sophia would make her choice to join the Rossar-mescro family the old-fashioned way, through marriage.

After two more years working together on their family barge and adding a baby boy to their numbers, Sophia made a decision to take one of the pieces from the jeweled items to a man in London who owned an auction house. He asked her how she came by such an exquisite thing and she told him it belonged to a dying friend she met on a boat coming from Romania.

The man shrugged. He wouldn't lose the commission from such a piece. Unfortunately, the poor postwar economy kept people's spending ability horribly restricted, but Sophia did well from the sale of her small treasure. She and Barty purchased two more barges for the family business. They hauled everything from apples to zinnias along England's canal system. The Rossar-mescros lived simply and freely. They kept their family and their small barges together because that is the Romani's way. It proved to be a successful plan indeed.

CHAPTER 9

Marsden-Lacey Constabulary
Present Day

CHIEF MERRIAM JOHNS WAS NOT happy. While he was off fishing in Scotland, someone further up the administrative ladder decided Marsden-Lacey's Constabulary needed some reorganization. Mainly, in the area of office allocation. Without informing him, his staff had moved him out of his office and dumped his things in a pile in the middle of another office not more than three doors down from where he'd been originally.

All morning, Johns had been raked over the coals at a public forum sponsored by the Marsden-Lacey Ladies Club regarding the performance of his staff and his constabulary. His mood was extremely foul when he arrived back at the constabulary. For at least ten minutes, he fumed about incompetence, time-wasters and the insanity of those further up the administrative food chain.

Raging and slamming things around in his 'new' office insured his crew kept their distance. The only exception was his new volunteer police cadet, Sam Berry. Sam was a young cadet with the Marsden-Lacey Constabulary. His mentor officer was Donna Waters and most days she had her work cut out for her keeping Sam focused and on task.

Sam's affection for the Chief, who he admired and saw as a father, meant he spent a good deal of his time following his mentor around. Johns for his part, was a reluctant father duck and preferred not to be bothered by anyone especially someone he considered a pimply-faced kid. Both were stubborn, but the office betting pool put odds on Sam. They knew Johns was made of gruff stuff on the outside but, like so many tough guys, somewhere in the middle, he was an old softy.

"Why are you so grumpy all the time, Chief?" Sam asked while leaning against the door jam of the Chief's new office. "You need to take up some kind of exercise. Might make a difference in your general well being."

"You know what would improve my general well being, Sam?" Johns asked with a hint of snippiness.

"Yeah, what?" Sam returned nonchalantly while checking the tidiness of his fingernails.

"You getting out of my office and finding something to do other than giving a man twice your age life advice!" Johns threw a full bag of rolled up sterile bandages from a drawer in his desk at Sam's head.

Unperturbed by the yelling or the bag bouncing off his cranium, Sam replied, "See. Grumpy."

"Get out of here!"

Sam jumped at John's deafening yell and bumped back into a solid something standing directly behind him. He turned around to see Donna's sour expression.

"The children are here from the preschool for their class visit. Go help Michael do the tour and when you're done, you can start the filing." Donna's tone was emphatic and all business. She was exceptionally adroit at handling children of any age. Even those still acting like children despite their advanced years sometimes benefited from her no-nonsense, honest approach.

Once Sam had shuffled down the hall grumbling about being on "diaper detail," Donna stepped into John's new office and focused on a bigger child.

"Here." She handed Johns two black sequined purses. "You had these in a file cabinet. Didn't think you would want the guys from headquarters to find them in your stuff."

John's eyebrows lifted practically off his forehead once he laid eyes on the purses. "Come on in here, Waters, and shut the door. We probably ought to talk."

Donna shut the door and shuffled around the mess on the floor to the seat the Chief pointed for her to take.

Johns peeked into one of the small black purse's interior and a happy sigh escaped him. "You're a good officer, Waters. Thank you for your attention to detail," he said with a meaningful look at the purse.

"Chief, better check your email. Nottingham Constabulary is sending a Detective Henry Richards up sometime this afternoon to talk with you about a murder. They sent a fax for you to sign acknowledging the two constabularies will be working together on the investigation."

Johns' mood went even darker. Why was Nottingham all of a sudden so interested in Marsden-Lacey? Office reassignments and new detectives muddling up his investigations were the last things he needed right now."

"Waters, I need some help getting this office organized before anyone gets here. Let me have that fax to sign and no interruptions until you see the whites of their eyes. Okay?"

"Not a problem, Chief. Want a cuppa?"

"Love one."

After Donna left, Johns scanned the room for a good hiding place. The scraggily, fake plant, a gift from his mother to "brighten up the place" would work perfectly. He lifted the plant by its stem revealing a nice-sized empty cavity. Shoving the purses into the bottom, he plopped the fake greenery back on top and neatly hid his whiskey-bottle-filled purses.

An hour flew by. With things tidy, Johns sat back in his comfy desk chair, eyed the wonky plant, and wondered if it was tea time yet. The day had been taxing but later he hoped to have a hardy dinner at The Traveller's and enjoy a pint, or two, depending on…

"Damn!" he said out loud. He wasn't going to The Traveller's tonight. He was going to the Roma camp. His mind jumped to the next thought: Martha.

"Forget The Traveller's," he said under his breath with a light smile playing around his eyes and mouth.

"Ummph." Someone cleared his throat.

Johns saw a plump, bald, badly-dressed man of about fifty smiling at him from the doorway. He presented his badge for Johns. After a few minutes of study, and finding all in order, Johns nodded.

"Detective Richards. Guess we're going to get to work together on this murder investigation. How's things in Nottingham?"

Chief Johns was eager to hear some gossip from another constabulary but Detective Richards didn't appear to be in the mood for tittle tattle.

"Yes, Sir. Nasty business. The woman, Sharon O'Connor, was forty-five, single, well liked in Nottingham and we can't find an enemy anywhere. She paid her bills on time, didn't drink other than a glass of wine here and there on special occasions. Recently, a background check was done in order for her to read to children once a week at one of the local preschools. Squeaky clean."

"How was she assaulted?" Johns asked.

"Nothing sexual but she was choked to death along the canal in Nottingham down by Clayton's Bridge and plopped into the canal. No one saw or heard anything that evening. We've talked to her family and colleagues but no one knows why she would have left her home so late at night. Her purse was left at home so it wasn't for money. I'm only left with a possible random act of violence or," he sighed heavily, "she had a lover. Can't even find a text message indicating she had one of those either."

"Why Marsden-Lacey?"

"That's my only lead. Her phone calendar showed she met with a man named Rossar-mescro. A Roma water traveler. The family has three boats and they skedaddled up here the day before she was found. She'd been in the water at least twenty-four hours so thought I'd pay them a visit. With your permission of course."

"Knew it. Knew it in my bones." Johns shook his head back and forth. "I've met with Rossar-mescro. He brought a document to a woman, Helen Ryes, who works in paper and book conservation. Wants her to tell him what it says. He mentioned another woman living in Nottingham who sent him here to talk with Ryes. Let's pull him in. I know where the water travelers are tied up along the canal."

Chief Johns and Sergeant Richards grabbed their coats and left for the section of the canal where narrowboaters liked to tether their floating homes along the bank. It was a nice location across from the old medieval Marsden-Lacey church of St. Elizabeth's and near the Barbel Bridge.

They drove the short distance to the area and walked the rest of the tow path until they reached the community of quiet narrowboat dwellers. As Johns and Detective Richards approached the area, they heard a woman cry out. Exchanging concerned expressions, they took off in the direction of the scream.

A young woman of about twenty-five came running toward them. Her dark hair was falling down her back and her face was blanched from fear. A group of people were running after her yelling for her to stop. As she got closer, Johns saw blood down her dress and on her hands. She locked her eyes on Johns and staggered. Clutching her middle torso, she crumpled into a heap on the ground.

Johns and Richards hurried to the woman. Signaling to Richards to stave off the crowd, Johns bent down and lifted the woman checking for the location of the wound. There in the area right below her rib cage, he saw the blood pumping out. She struggled to say something.

"Baba's sword. Baba's sword," she whispered with frantic eyes.

As he applied pressure to the wound, he said, "Hold on, dear. Stay with me. It's going to be okay."

Johns dialed the emergency number and, in a professional manner, detailed where they were and what he needed. The young woman went limp and jerked.

A man broke through the crowd of people and rushed forward. It was Stephan Rossar-mescro. Falling to the ground, he grabbed the young woman's hand.

"Laura, Laura. Please, please…" His voice trailed off into sobbing as he bent over her still body.

Johns sensed when her spirit passed. On more than one occasion, he'd been witness to death and its nuances.

"Who is she?" Johns asked Stephan.

"My daughter!" he cried. "Oh, dear God! My child."

CHAPTER 10

THE AMBULANCE ARRIVED AND SO did the rest of the police force along with the forensic team. Since Laura Rossar-mescro was dead, the forensic team was in charge. The Chief and Detective Richards started the questioning.

Stephan Rossar-mescro was the first person they needed to talk to. The poor man was in complete agony and wouldn't leave her body. It took a solid hour before Johns, Richards and one of the other constables were able to get the family to step away from the body and to understand the necessity of not touching her. Once this was achieved and the rest of the Rossar-mescros returned to their boats, Johns and Richards escorted the broken Stephan to a place where their conversation would be undisturbed.

"Do you know who did this, Mr. Rossar-mescro?" Johns asked gently.

The man, who earlier that day was vital and happy at the constabulary, appeared ten years older. "No, no, no. No one would kill Laura. She was beautiful and good."

"Sir, someone did this in the middle of the day with all of your family around. Were there any problems, jealousies or arguments happening amongst your people?" Johns pushed on.

Stephan was quiet, staring down into the palms of his hands. He didn't even acknowledge the idea of the murder being instigated within his family. Instead, he became reflective. “We saw a man today. I saw him before staring at us from way up high on the bridge.”

Johns shook his head. “Where?”

With a shaking hand, Stephan pointed to the stone bridge crossing the canal below St. Elizabeth’s.

Quiet for another short moment, he finally said, “One night, my Laura saw a man watching us from Clayton’s Bridge in Nottingham. She pointed him out and said Baba Sophia told her he had evil in his soul.”

Johns understood and respected the strong belief among the Romani community that their ancestors remained attached to the family providing guidance and protection even after death. He needed solid facts though, not intangible ones.

“Did you see him, too, that night?”

“Not clearly. I saw a figure in the dark standing there. I didn’t see a face.”

“Did Laura know him?” Detective Richards intervened with his question.

“No. She didn’t know him.” Stephan studied them like they were crazy to ask such a question.

“Do you think it was the same man today? Did she talk with him?”

“Not exactly. She pointed him out to me. He was watching us.”

“I need a description, Mr. Rossar-mescro,” Johns said, “would you know the man if you saw him again?”

“I don’t know. He was wearing a black coat, black trousers and a stocking cap pulled down around his head.”

“Mr. Rossar-mescro, I will have my Sergeant Michael Endicott take your full statement. Please wait here.”

Turning to Richards, he said, "Come on. Let's go see where this happened."

As Johns and Detective Richards walked away, Richards whispered, "Do you think it was a hate crime against the Romani?"

Johns replied, "No, I don't. They're peaceful people. We've got two dead women. Question is, how are they connected?"

The two policemen walked farther down to where three well-maintained narrowboats lay quietly against the canal's embankment. Two children sat on a man's lap holding onto his sweater and staring with large, round eyes at Richards and Johns.

"Are you one of the Rossar-mescros?" Johns called loudly.

The man nodded yes.

"He doesn't have words," one of the children said. "He uses his hands to talk."

Johns took a deep breath and let it out. Heads peeked out of back doors and windows of the three boats. First, Johns saw a young boy's face and an older woman's. Slowly, the Rossar-mescro family reemerged from their floating homes. Not a single one of them appeared to be inclined to conversation, but Johns' twenty-some years in the force meant he was comfortable handling a crowd.

"Does anyone here know anything about the attack? I will be needing statements from everyone, but it would be a great help, if you have information, to come forward."

Watching and waiting, Johns soon got the picture. Not a single person made a move to say anything, instead they stared past Johns and Richards to the figure of Stephan Rossar-mescro coming down the tow path.

The Romani wouldn't talk until they were given the sign it was okay from their paterfamilias.

Once the older man arrived, Johns said, "Mr. Rossar-mescro, you need to let your family know if they have any information, they need to share it with the police. This is a serious crime we've got on our hands. I know this is a terrible thing to happen to you, but if the murderer is close by, we need information to catch them."

Stephan studied Johns' face for a brief minute. Turning to his family, he said, "Laura has been killed. If you saw anything, tell this man. He's honest and fair."

With that statement, the entire group of water travelers talked at once.

"Wait, wait a minute!" Johns' voice raised over the chorus of people all trying to talk at once.

"One at a time, please. Let's start with this lady." Johns pointed to a small, older woman of about seventy. "Madam, who are you and did you see anything?"

The wizened face gave nothing away. She pursed her lips and, taking a deep breath, said, "I am Miri, Stephan's sister. Laura saw a man sitting on the other side of the water." She pointed to the place Stephan had earlier indicated. "Laura told him she knew why he was a hunter. She said Baba told her he was a shade come to take something that wasn't his. I heard her tell him to go away."

"Anyone else see the man or talk with him?" Detective Richards asked.

The remainder of the party shook their heads back and forth. Johns knew that it was a living, breathing person since both Stephan and Miri had seen him. The Romani communicated things differently.

The boy sitting on the mute's lap climbed down and pointed to the soccer field laying adjacent to the tow path they stood on. "Laura walked over to the field. There. She was gone for a long time but she came back through the grass over by the big wheel."

Johns peered down the tow path to see the old abandoned mill house lying on the same side as where both Miri and Stephan indicated seeing the man watching the Romani. "One last question. Is anything missing?"

The child spoke one last time. "In her hand, there was something long and bright. It glittered in the sun. She went to fight the hunter."

"Baba's sword?" Johns asked almost more to himself than to the others listening.

The old woman narrowed her eyes at the words Johns uttered. She crossed herself muttering something about greed and ghosts. She raised her hand at the others to focus their attention on what she would say next. They waited for her words.

"Baba Sophia's sword must be found. No stone unturned until it's back with the Rossar-mescros. No stone unturned."

Johns, at her words, tensed. The last thing he needed was a family of Romani running around the country digging under people's flower pots and in their garden sheds trying to find a long, deadly knife.

"Mrs. Rossar-mescro, we don't want your family searching for this man or for the sword. He's dangerous. Let the police do their work and we'll find your family's heirloom. Will you give me a description of it?" He turned to Stephan for an answer.

"It was long and slightly curved. There was a gold handle. It's been in our family for almost a hundred years and was my Baba's, or as you say, grandmother's. It *was* our good luck piece."

Stephan's demeanor changed as he talked. He was pensive and in a burst of oration for everyone to hear, he said, "The sword took one of our own. It's turned on our family. No one must keep it, if they find it. Give it to this man." He pointed at Johns. Turning to the Chief, he continued, "There's a curse now on that blade. It will bring only darkness and death. No Rossar-mescro will be stung by its poison again. The blade and the paper are brothers. One will try and find the other and evil haunts the person who handles either."

The group was quiet. A gurgle and humming slowly emanated from the old woman, Miri, who earlier called for the sword to be found. She stared into the sky as if in a trance and her body became rigid. Like a Greek oracle from old, Miri's voice boomed from her fragile body with this warning:

"A Helen holds the letter.
A hunter wields the blade.
Death creeps among us,
A debt is finally paid."

CHAPTER 11

MARTHA AND HELEN PULLED UP in front of the veterinary office a few minutes before five o'clock. Amos was coming home and Martha was trying to prepare herself emotionally to see the tiny invalid.

"Helen, when we see Amos for the first time, whatever you do, don't laugh. She's sensitive about her appearance and this may be an extremely humbling experience for her ego."

"It's a dog, Martha."

"Helen! I'm not going to argue the notion that she isn't human. She's better!"

In a bit of a huff and feeling indignant by the tone of Helen's dog comment, Martha grabbed a pink baby blanket from the back of her car and made her way into the vet's office with Helen coming up behind.

The girls waited in the reception area until one of the assistants came out of the back holding a cone-wearing Amos. All four legs were shaved except for the paws, which had been left with long fur patches giving the pint-sized dog the appearance of wearing baggy socks. Small scrapes and bruises were along her shaved sides and a large pink bandage weaved and wrapped its way around her chest, back and front shoulder. Amos' tail was wonky and naked except for some fluff still wobbling at the tip.

When the patient saw Martha, the once fuzzy tail wagged feebly in recognition. Martha's maternal heart experienced a strong thump of pity and love.

She went over to the pathetic dog and wrapped her gently in the pink blanket. "It's going to be okay, Fuzzy-pants. I've got lots of treats for you at home," her voice heavy with emotion.

Amos wagged her tail even harder and shot a glance at the exit in a worried way.

"Don't worry, we're going home. Helen, would you please pay for me? I'm taking Amos out to the car."

Helen took Martha's purse, paid, and drove them home. When they arrived, Johns was waiting in his car parked by the garden wall of Flower Pot Cottage. He came over to Martha's door and opened it. There, in Martha's arms, was a plastic cone wrapped in a pink blanket. Deep within the cone's recess were two coal-black eyes and one black nose.

"Girls, let me help you inside. I have something to tell you," he said.

Martha detected from his tone that it wasn't something good. She hustled in through the garden gate and turned to see Johns scanning the area and waiting for Helen to lock up the car. Once Helen was through the gate Johns followed her indoors.

With the front door locked, Johns said he wanted to check the house and asked the girls to stay in the living room.

"What on Earth is this all about, Merriam?" Martha demanded.

Johns turned to see three sets of blinking eyes waiting for an answer. "I don't want to worry you but I have reason to believe someone is searching for Helen and that person may be dangerous."

Martha and Helen stared dumbfoundedly at Johns.

"What the heck is going on? Dangerous person? Helen, why would anyone want to hurt you?" Martha shifted her gaze back and forth between Johns and Helen then stopped as if some truth dawned on her. "That was a dumb thing to say. Just two months ago someone was trying to ice you. What is it with you and people wanting to mess you up?"

"How should I know! You haven't stopped rambling long enough for the Chief to tell me. Give the man a chance to finish. Please!" Helen said, exasperated.

They both took deep breaths and exhaled forcefully. Giving Johns their full attention, they raised their eyebrows and waited for him to explain.

"Helen, the documents Stephan Rossar-mescro gave you, do you still have them?" Johns asked.

"Yes, I do. They're in my briefcase."

"Good, I'll be taking them as evidence in a murder investigation," he replied.

"Murder? Who's dead?" Martha demanded.

Johns paused and studied the two women. "Helen do you know a woman named Sharon O'Connor? She lived in Nottingham."

"Yes, I know Sharon. Please, please tell me it isn't her you're investigating?"

Johns nodded. “I’m sorry Helen. It’s Sharon. She was murdered about forty-eight hours ago. Can’t be specific with the time yet.”

Martha put Amos on the couch and laid a hand on Helen’s shoulder. “Would you like a cup of tea, Helen? Here, have a seat and I’ll run in the kitchen and make us all one.”

“Martha, stay put for a moment,” Johns said in a firm tone. “I need to check around and I’d like it if both of you are in the same place. I’ve got Sergeant Endicott outside sweeping the area and in a minute we’ll all have a chat. Okay?”

The girls said they would wait. While Johns searched the rooms, Helen and Martha sat subdued on the couch.

“You okay, Helen?” Martha asked in a low voice.

“Oh, Martha. Not really. She was a friend and an excellent colleague. Why would anyone want to kill Sharon?”

“What kind of work did she do?”

“She owned an antique store and dealt in rare books, prints and miniatures,” Helen replied.

“Do you think the document might have something to do with it?”

“No idea, but why would Sharon send the letter to me?”

“Was she an honest sort of person?”

“I think so. She was one of those people who liked to help out in areas she enjoyed. Kind of an eccentric, but definitely a professional.”

"If she sent the document to you, she must have thought it was something deserving of special care or of unique importance. Don't you think?" Martha asked.

"The only reason I can think of Sharon would send it to me is she wanted it authenticated or perhaps she recognized its value and wanted a second opinion."

"When you studied it, was there something special about it?"

"No, other than it was old," Helen replied. "It was written in Russian. I won't know more until a friend of mine in Nottingham has a chance to see it. One thing though that stood out. There was a list on the document, and I had the feeling it corresponded some how with the boats belonging to the Romani people."

Johns came back into the room and the girls stopped talking.

"Find anything of interest upstairs?" Martha asked.

Johns smiled. "The house is safe."

"Safe enough for me to go make some tea?" Martha stood up.

A loud knock came at the front door making Amos bark and everyone else jump except Johns. The dog's cone slightly quivered from the low guttural sound emanating from the broken but brave protector of hearth and home. Johns walked over and opened the door and Amos wobbled over to sniff at Michael Endicott, one of the leading lights of the Marsden-Lacey Constabulary force.

"Nothing to report, Chief," Michael said. "But there are signs along the back kitchen window of someone trying to break in. Also, someone's been smoking back and forth along the canal side of the garden wall. The butts are new ones, probably only one or two days old."

Martha spoke up at the news. "Someone's been out there? That must be why Amos was so agitated yesterday when she ran out in front of your car. She whined and scratched at the door all morning on Tuesday. That's not normal unless she thinks something or someone is outside. I thought it was because the wind was blowing things around."

"Are you thinking that someone is watching the cottage, Chief?" Helen asked.

"Yes," Johns answered. "The Romani made no secret of their intent to come find you. Michael, pick up a few of the butts and get them to forensics."

Turning to Martha and Helen, he said, "Ladies, want to come stay at the farm for a while? Mum would love to have the company. We've loads of room. She's busy with her garden planning these days but she's one incredible cook."

Martha shook her head. "I don't think that would work. What about Amos? Would your mother be okay with pets?"

Johns frowned. "If you stay here, I can't guarantee your safety unless I put men around the house twenty-four seven. That's not in my budget." He thought a moment and smiled rakishly. "There's always your former accommodations at the jail."

"Not happening," Martha and Helen said in unison. They both laughed and said to the other, "You owe me dinner!"

"Hey, quit clowning around. This is serious. Bring the dog, bring the cats. I've got lots of mice for them to catch."

The girls shrugged.

"If your mother tells us it's okay, we would do it," Helen said.

"Fair enough. Give me a second to call her."

He walked away down the hall and a few minutes later he handed the phone to Helen.

"Mrs. Johns? Yes, this Helen Ryes. We don't want to inconvenience you…"

Everyone watched Helen's face as she talked with Polly Johns. She smiled and quickly shot a glance at Chief Johns like she was hearing some juicy morsel of information. Laughing, she said, "We would love to come over. Thank you so much for your hospitality. Yes, I promise to bring my parcheesi board."

Helen handed the phone back to Johns.

"Yes, Mum. I'm going to tell them you like to play for big stakes and you're not as innocent as you try to appear. We should be there in about an hour."

Chief Johns ended his call. "Girls, how about you get packed."

Helen's face drained of color and she pointed down the hall to the window.

Johns turned in time to see a white face peering in the corner pane of glass before it vanished. "Go, Mike, and take the front way. I'm out the back."

The men moved like cats, quietly and quickly out of the room, leaving Helen and Martha holding on to each other. Amos went berserk barking. Gus and Vera, the two cats who had been curled up in their favorite chair together, scuttled out of the living room and up the stairs.

"I'm not waiting around here to be shot or stabbed. I'm going to get my stud stick upstairs," Martha said.

"Your what?" Helen exclaimed.

"My stud stick," Martha said nonchalantly. "You know, the cricket bat I've got upstairs?"

"Why on God's green earth is it called a stud stick?" Helen asked.

"Well, because you have to be kind of a stud, or tough guy, to handle it," Martha said cockily while standing there with one hand on her hip.

"I tell you what, Martha. If you try and leave me to go up and retrieve your so-called stud stick, you might find me bowling a beamer at you with that house shoe over there."

Martha nudged the shoe with her foot. "What's a beamer?"

"Ask your guy. He'd know."

After a few frustrating minutes of wondering what the men were finding outside, Martha convinced Helen it would be okay to get their overnight bags ready. Happy with any excuse to quit standing around like fish in a barrel, the girls went upstairs and packed.

Coming back down, Helen remembered she was supposed to meeting Piers. "Fudge! I forgot about Piers. He's supposed to be meeting me on the Barbel Bridge."

Glancing at her watch, she said, "Oh, no. He's probably there. I've got to call him."

Helen picked up her cell phone and dialed Piers' number. No answer, so she left a message asking him to call.

Johns and Michael stomped into the house. The Chief's face was blotchy with anger.

"Are you ready, ladies? I'd like to leave immediately."

"What happened?" Helen asked.

"Whoever it was used the canal to escape. They must have a boat. We just heard a motor and because it's dark, we were only able to see the silhouette of a person in a motor craft going up the canal. Let's make haste and get you both out to the farm."

"Which way did he go, Chief?" Martha asked.

"Towards Barbel Bridge."

"Piers!" the girls said together.

Helen's phone rang and it was Piers. She quickly hit accept.

"Piers? Are you on the bridge?" Helen asked hurriedly. She nodded to the others that he was indeed on the bridge.

"Do you see anyone coming up the river in a small powerboat?"

No one in the room moved. Their gazes focused on Helen's face. She nodded. "He can hear a small motor in the distance but definitely coming toward him. Piers, if you get a chance to see the person, try and use your phone to take a photo, okay?"

Johns countermanded her request, "No! Tell him to not draw any attention to himself, but if at all possible to see where the person goes. I'm going to the constabulary to get Sergeant Cross. We'll cover the two roads on the bridge."

Helen reiterated exactly what the Chief had said and hit end on her phone. "He says he'll do it and will call us."

"Ladies, I want you to follow Michael to the farm. I've got Mr. Cousins' phone number. I'll see you hopefully later this evening. Mum will be waiting for you."

Martha and Helen nodded yes and watched Johns leave. Once he was gone, Martha turned to Helen and said, "Let's give Michael the slip and go to Barbel Bridge. What do you say?"

Helen gave her a wicked smile and answered, "You do like the adventurous life, don't you?"

"It's in my blood now, Helen. Up for some excitement? We'll stay very discrete. They'll never know we're there."

"Let's go. We'll take my car. It's bigger so we'll have more room for the zoo and our luggage," Helen replied.

Helen and Martha grabbed the cats and their overnight bags. Amos was tucked into her blanket again and once they were in the car, they gave Michael the sign they would follow him.

The cars pulled out together. About halfway out of the village, Helen slowed down enough to let another car get in between her and Michael's police vehicle. When they reached a stoplight, Helen again hung back and Michael pulled through but the girls' car had to wait, effectively distancing themselves even more.

"Let's back track to the bridge and see what's up," Martha said.

As they approached the area, they saw the Barbel Bridge but it was quiet as death. Not a soul was in sight and the few street lights were too feeble to illuminate the area clearly. Stopping the car at the edge of the road, they scanned the landscape for signs of life.

"No one, anywhere. What do you make of it?" Helen asked in an almost whisper.

Martha didn't get a chance to answer. Three men dressed in black from head to toe, scrambled up the side of the embankment. They were dragging a fourth man along in front of them, hunched over and barely walking.

The girls gasped.

Helen whispered frantically, "It's Piers! What do we do? Where's the Chief?"

"He's probably watching from somewhere or waiting for backup. Give it a minute."

They watched as the men dragged Piers up to the top of the bridge and talked among themselves. With the men illuminated by the light from the bridge lamps, Martha and Helen saw the shoulder holsters tightly fitted to their chests.

"They're going to kill him, Martha. We've got to do something."

"Ram 'em, Helen. Turn the car on and hit the accelerator. Go in with your horn blaring."

Helen's head jerked around with an expression of horror on her face. "What?'

"You heard me. I've got my stick and I'll jump out and nail 'em. Hurry! They're laying him over the railing!"

Helen flipped on her lights, punched the gas and laid on the horn. As the car jolted forward, Helen and Martha screamed and Amos barked in chorus. The men turned around, dropping Piers who lay in a heap on the pavement.

The car roared up onto the bridge and the men, completely startled by the sudden arrival of a flying black Mercedes, turned and began to ran.

"Yeah! Run you creeps!" Martha yelled.

She rolled down the window and brandished her stud stick, hitting one running man in the head. He tucked and rolled. The rest of the men ran down the other side of the bridge and jumped into a car. Helen hit her brakes and turned around in her seat. She put the car in reverse and pressing the gas hard, she went backwards to where Piers lay along the wall.

The car's brakes squealed as she came to a stop. The girls jumped out. Martha ran over to the man still lying on the ground and hit him again on the back. He groaned but went limp. Suddenly, two Volvos arrived and Sergeant Cross jumped out of a car and an angry Chief Johns came marching toward Martha who stood next to her bad-guy trophy.

"What the hell are you doing?" he yelled.

"I'm saving Piers from being killed," Martha said with a proud swing of her cricket bat.

Chief Johns went over to Martha and stared down at the man on the ground.

"Knocked him in the head going about thirty miles an hour. I think he's out for a while." Martha tapped the bat on the tip of her high heel shoe and smiled cheekily.

"You're not in the old American wild west, Littleword. You're going to have to come in for assault with a deadly weapon," Johns said shaking his head.

"Chief!" Cross called. "We've got an ambulance coming. They're setting up a road block along the two main roads leaving the village."

Johns turned away from Martha. "You know you are in legal trouble? Do you have a good solicitor?"

"I stopped a man from being killed. Where the hell were you? And yes, I do know a very good solicitor. Calling her right now."

"Bringing the Calvary is where I've been, Littleword. Sorry, I wasn't here to see you in action."

"I'll let you get on with your job, Officer."

"Chief," Johns said firmly.

Martha gave him a wink and a nod then began dialing a number on her phone and walked away toward Helen's car.

Johns watched her confident retreat and the sashay of her backside. Averting his eyes and forcing his unwilling brain to shift gears, he said, "Good. Let's get this guy cuffed."

He walked over to Helen and Piers who were sitting on the ground. Piers sported a couple of cuts and bruises on his face. Helen sat beside him holding his hand.

"Mr. Cousins are you okay to talk?" Johns asked.

"Chief, call me Piers. I think we've been through enough that we can be on a first-name basis, don't you?"

"Let's get you up, Cousins. Did you have a chance to hear anything the assailants said?"

"They were speaking Russian. At least I'm pretty sure it was Russian. I couldn't make anything out. Wish I could be more help, Chief."

Martha, done with her phone call, joined them.

Johns gave Piers a hand and got him to his feet. He turned to Helen and Martha.

"I don't know how to communicate with you both. You defy orders, you throw yourself into dangerous situations, get in the way of police procedures and as if these weren't enough to deal with, you've assaulted a man. His friends will come back and that's where it gets sticky for you."

"I'm hungry," Martha said. "We'd better not make your mother wait on us any longer. She said she was making a pork roast."

The three gaped at Martha like she was a crazy woman.

"What? I've not eaten since noon and it's seven o'clock."

Piers walked over to the paramedic who checked out his wounds while Helen peeked into her car.

She said, "I think we'd better get our zoo over to the farm, Martha, or take them for a short walk. Your menagerie would be happier anywhere but in my backseat."

"Yep, let's go. Merriam, can we give our statements tomorrow? I want my solicitor present," Martha asked Chief Johns.

"No."

"Excuse me," Martha said. "My solicitor has asked that I wait until she is present to discuss my actions this evening. That goes for Helen, too."

A smile played along the corner of Johns' mouth. "Okay, Mrs. Ryes and Mrs. Littleword. Tomorrow meet me with your solicitor at the constabulary for a statement but until then, please get to the farm. My mother is not happy waiting for people once she's cooked them dinner."

Johns scanned the busy surroundings of the bridge. "Michael! Come here!" he yelled.

Michael came over and grimaced at Helen and Martha.

"You girls want me to lose my job?" he asked.

Feeling contrite, they said, "Sorry, Sergeant Endicott."

Put out with men being bossy and needy, Martha opened her car door and settled herself inside. Turning to both Johns and Michael, she said, "If we hadn't come over here, Piers would no doubt be dead." Shutting the door hard, Martha put an end to any further debate on the subject.

Helen got in the car and turned the key. The engine hummed into life and they drove the entire way to Polly Johns' home following Michael's car at a perfect distance.

"You know what makes me want to scream, Helen?" Martha asked finally, breaking her ten minute silence.

"What?"

"Not one single person said, 'Nice job, girls. Way to jump in and fearlessly save your friend's life.'"

As Martha talked, she got more ramped up and dramatic. "We were amazing, Helen. You drove this car like a stunt driver!"

Helen nodded in agreement and turned to Martha. They both raised their eyebrows and their faces broke out in big, wide-open grins. For the rest of the drive, they relived their crazy moment on the bridge causing much wild laughter and the occasional good humored screaming fits.

It was a happy but tired crowd who finally pulled into Polly's gate. They ate a delicious meal, slept snuggled under big, fluffy duvets and dreamed their own fantastical version of the evening's experience.

For the men, who later in the deep of the night, came lurking again around Martha's Flower Pot Cottage, they found flyers taped to a few of the windows saying:

"The women are gone. The document isn't here. It's at the Police Station. Come on by. Be happy to show you around." - Chief M. Johns

CHAPTER 12

EARLY THE NEXT MORNING POLLY was busy in the wonderful old inglenook kitchen making a hearty farm breakfast of eggs, toast, sausages, and fresh ground coffee. Johns' mother was never happier than when she was hosting, cooking or brewing beer.

Martha's nose woke her up, so she quickly dressed and grabbed Amos. First things first, a fresh morning stroll for Amos to scout the outside perimeter and a quick check on the cats who'd been tucked into one of the barn stalls the previous night.

The morning air was so fresh and crisp that Martha stood for a long moment drinking in the view and breathing deeply. The Johns farm was rural England at its most charming and beautiful. Rolling pastures, medieval farm buildings and old brick stables beguiled the eye and brain into thoughts of a bucolic history only an anglophile can summon up in their mind.

Martha had removed Amos' medical cone for her walk. The dog's pleasure was clear with all the sniffing and snorting she made at all the smells her nose turned up. They came through the huge doors of the old barn and headed toward the stalls. Martha saw an older woman bending down and petting her cat, Gus.

"He's a love. Never met a stranger," Martha said in a friendly manner to the woman. Gus threaded in between the legs of the standing lady.

"Your cat likes his new home," the woman said.

Martha cocked her head, thought for a moment and, laughing, asked, "Did he tell you it's only a bed and breakfast?"

"No, he told me he loved the smell of all the mice and the hay. Your other cat is scared and won't come out of the stall. I tried to give her a bite of my egg but she won't have anything to do with it," the woman said.

"You're so good with animals," Martha said. "Do you live here, too?"

The old woman didn't answer Martha's question, instead she said, "I've got to get back. My family is waiting for breakfast. A bit of advice about the black cat still hiding in the stall. She lost her first mother and she needs to be told by you that you will not leave her behind. Okay? You understand?"

Martha's eyes locked with the woman's. She understood perfectly. "I most definitely will do that. Thank you. Can I know your name, please?"

"Miri. My name is Miri."

She whispered something to the cats and Gus mewed loudly and rolled over on his back playfully.

Martha was surprised by Gus' behavior. "I've never seen him do that for anyone but me."

"I told them they had a good human to watch over them and they needed to stay put, not run away. I must go. Have a good day."

She watched Miri head out over the pasture and, in a few minutes, disappear below the rise of the hill.

Scene Break

WHEN HELEN CAME DOWNSTAIRS, POLLY was laughing and having a conversation with two men. As she got closer to the kitchen, the smells of breakfast tantalized her nose reminding her of her aunt's wonderful southern cooking.

"Good morning!" Helen beamed at the spread on the long farm table. There, warmly ensconced in two comfy wingback chairs on either side of the solid Aga stove, were Perigrine Clark and Alistair Turner. The two of them smiled cheerfully at Helen and got up to shake her hand.

"Why, Mrs. Ryes, how are you? We heard you're being hunted by gangsters? Scared much?" Alistair asked coolly.

Polly pursed her lips tightly and turned back to the stove busying herself with a pot of something in the oven.

"Well, I didn't know they were gangsters," Helen said, starting to lose her appetite.

"Oh, dear, don't pay any attention to these two busybodies. They were at the post office this morning and heard about the excitement last night. Grimsy was up at the crack of dawn this morning, getting the villagers acquainted with your daring exploits, Mrs. Ryes," Polly said, clanking around on the Aga.

"There's a neighborhood crime watch meeting to take place at the Village Community Center tomorrow. We hope you'll come and tell your story," Perigrine said.

"Yes, I think Martha and I would both like that very much. Thank you."

Polly bustled over and put more biscuits on the table. "Dear, you take your mind off those Romani for a while and eat something. You're too thin. Eat! You don't need to bother with that silly neighborhood watch meeting tomorrow. They're a bunch of nosey busybodies, if you ask me." Polly gave Perigrine and Alistair the evil eye. She put down some honey on the table and busied herself with digging in the pantry for marmalade.

"Polly," Perigrine said in a diplomatic tone, "of course we want these two brave women to come talk to our Neighborhood Watch meeting. They epitomize the kind of take charge, fearless attitude more villagers should aspire to."

"I want to shake that man's hand," Martha declared from the kitchen doorway. She continued into the big room with Amos wobbling at her heels. "You are obviously an excellent judge of character."

Perigrine bowed elegantly to Martha and replied in a stately manner, "And you, good woman, are a rare example of spirit in the face of menacing evil."

Polly said, "Okay, if we are all done with spreading the fertilizer around, how about we eat."

Scene Break

ONCE THE GUESTS WERE DONE with the delicious breakfast and enjoying their coffee around the long oak table in Polly's kitchen, Perigrine and Alistair managed to extract all the gossip about the Romani family, the mysterious document and how the same document may need to be translated by a man in Nottingham named Albright. The back door was open to the walled garden for fresh air, so Amos, fat from feasting on bacon, was contentedly sunning her motley furred body in a sun patch that streamed in through the door.

"Where did you learn to make southern biscuits, Mrs. Johns?" Helen asked. "They are like the ones my Aunt Stacey made when we visited her in Biloxi."

"First of all, dear, my name is Polly. Yorkshire people do prefer a respectful reserve when it comes to calling elders by their surnames, but once someone sleeps under my roof, I don't hold with that notion. It's Polly, plain and simple."

"There was nothing plain and simple about these biscuits," Martha added. She was liberally buttering her second one. "The last time I ate a biscuit this light was at a cafe in Mountain View, Arkansas. Barely room for six tables in the whole place with a line of people running out through the door waiting to get in for breakfast."

Martha took a deep, satisfied sigh. "Polly, I want to learn how to make these."

"That can be arranged," Polly said beaming. She'd been watching Martha in short, furtive ways all morning trying to access her. A mother's keen sense told her there was a good reason why these women were housed here for safe keeping when it would have been just as easy for Merriam to put them in protective custody elsewhere.

She ruled out Helen the minute she laid eyes on her. Elegant, classically pretty, academically minded and a smidgen uptight, she seemed an unlikely candidate for her son's affections. The redhead, on the other hand, was the type who would make Merriam want to pull his hair out. She was saucy, opinionated, and had curves like a Scottish Highland's switchback road. It was pure chemistry, and if Polly understood one thing well as a brewer, it was chemistry.

"I learned to make those biscuits from a friend of mine," Polly said. "She married an American serviceman and went home to Athens, Georgia with him. His mother taught her cookery. For thirty years, when she comes home to visit her sisters, she always spends a few days with me and we make something from her southern repertoire. Last year I learned to make Mississippi Mud Cake. I thought Merriam was going to eat the entire pan."

"Let Helen and I do dinner some night," Martha said. "That is if you don't mind having people messing about in your kitchen?"

"Martha, I would love to have someone else cook a meal in this kitchen besides me for once. Don't expect Merriam to be on time," Polly said with a hint of irritation in her voice.

Shifting her gaze to the two impeccably dressed men, Alistair and Perigrine, tidily folding their napkins, she said, "Would you boys like to come to dinner tonight? Helen, you invite someone, too. I think I would like to have a small dinner party. Everyone bring something fun to eat and share."

The room burst in excited exchanges of ideas and laughter. Martha and Helen wanted to make jambalaya and cornbread hushpuppies while P. and Alistair, in keeping with the southern-cajun theme, were going to bring the cocktails. Polly promised to do dessert.

Around eight thirty, as they all dispersed from the kitchen to go their separate ways, Martha remembered to ask about her pets. "Polly, if I leave Amos and the cats in your barn today, will they be okay? Your helper this morning said my cat was nervous about my abandoning her. I wanted to make sure they weren't able to get out, if the doors were shut."

Polly turned to Martha with a perplexed expression. "I don't have a helper here on the farm. We don't keep big animals anymore or do any farming. Who did you talk to?"

"She called herself Miri. A nice older woman. She was sitting in your barn but said she needed to get back to her family for breakfast. I'm sorry. I should have mentioned it."

Polly tugged on Perigrine's jacket. "Come on. I might need some back-up. I want to check on my chickens."

The group followed the short, but stalwart Polly out to the old timbered barn. It was empty except the cats. In the farm yard, the chickens pecked around and scampered off in different directions as the humans came tramping through.

"I'll check my hen house," Polly said.

Once inside she realized she wouldn't have fresh eggs for breakfast tomorrow. "I've been cleaned out. Probably also need to check my brewery. Eggs are one thing but if someone's been thieving from my brewery…"

The brewhouse was undisturbed. Whoever took the eggs wasn't interested in the beer.

"Merriam will need to know about this," Polly said irritably. "Did you see which way the woman went, Martha?"

"Oh, yes. She went over the pasture." Martha pointed toward the area she saw Miri travel.

"There's nothing in that direction except the river Calder. I might hike down that way and see what I can see," Polly said. With a wave to the others still standing in a semi-circle, she headed off across the farm yard and to the unseen river lying below the rise in the land.

They watched her go. Helen and Martha said they would see the others tonight and waved goodbye as well.

Left alone in the farmyard with Perigrine, Alistair toed one of the curious advancing chickens with one of his timelessly fashionable Grenson brogues. The nosey chicken arched her neck in readiness to peck the leather obstacle but instead halted her forward motion and cocked her head to one side for a better view of the boot's elegant lines and perforations. Acknowledging the shoe's good breeding, the peckish hen turned around abruptly and toddled off seemingly abashed as a chicken can be at her own lack of footwear.

"P. do you remember the Romani people we met in Poland a few years ago?" Alistair asked.

Perigrine kicked an imaginary clod of dirt with the toe of his shoe and contemplated the miniature figure of the retreating Polly. "I do, Ally. I remember them quite well. We discussed this yesterday."

"Do you remember the story they told us?"

"Been trying to remember the exact details since breakfast," Perigrine said.

"Thought so."

"The letter in Russian must be the key, Perigrine," Alistair said walking out of the yard with Perigrine following him. "I think we should get all the information we can. I don't want there to be murder number three. I wonder if our good Chief of Police would welcome some assistance with the letter?"

They were quiet for a while as they found their way into the walled garden where Polly wished to grow a variety of plants to improve her beer brewing.

"Offering your assistance is the only way you'll be able to lay eyes on it," Perigrine said. He used a digital laser machine to measure the enclosure, writing numbers down in a small sketch book.

Alistair, using a small spade, scooped up some of the garden's dirt and put it into a bag for testing later.

"Yes, and I think we should move on this today. Better we take care of this, Perigrine, than letting it get out of hand. I think you know who's probably involved. Uncivilized brutes masquerading as heroes. Worst kind of people. You heard what Helen said about calling Albright in Nottingham."

Neither talked for a while. They were busy mulling over in their minds the best way to proceed.

"By the way, what did you have in mind to bring for tonight's dinner party?" Perigrine asked.

"Oh, I thought a cocktail of Death in the Afternoon," Alistair smiled knowingly and turned away.

"Daring drink, my friend."

Perigrine studied the back of Alistair's head wondering whether Alistair's good taste dictated the choice of cocktail or if something more dark was the motivation.

Alistair headed to where their car was parked but halted his stride. He turned around to see Perigrine studying him. Alistair smiled in that enigmatic way he had when he meant exactly the opposite of what he said.

"P., dear, it's purely a question of the drink complementing the meal. No double entendres. Only an attempt at living the best life possible. I'm sure it's what we both want, of course."

"Of course," Perigrine agreed and being done with their measurements, they headed to the village. Alistair wanted to have a chat with Chief Johns.

CHAPTER 13

ONCE THEY LEFT THE JOHNS' farm, the girls went to Flower Pot Cottage to quickly change cars. Martha wanted to be behind the wheel for a while and Helen wanted some time to look over the data base they'd been working on for The Grange.

As Martha's Mini Cooper, which she called the Green Bean, zipped along Marsden-Lacey's quaint back streets, the sky began to turn cloudy. Reaching the High Street, she shifted down into third gear, hit the accelerator and practically catapulted their craft up the old cobblestone road toward the summit.

With driving panache, Martha expertly maneuvered the compact vehicle in between a few pedestrians, two lorries parked awkwardly along the entrance area and one motorcyclist wearing an egg-shaped helmet towing a small cart with what appeared to be his laundry. She pulled into the parking lot of The Grange and with incredibly deft handling of her steering wheel, parked the Green Bean neatly between a posh BMW and a sedate, but respectable sedan.

"Perfect timing. Exactly nine o'clock on the dot," Martha said.

"I would ask why you have to drive that way every single place we go, but honestly, I'm beginning to think it's because you have a death wish," Helen said after she extricated herself from the tiny toy-mobile. Wobbling slightly, she adjusted her collar, made sure her pearls were hanging evenly and pulled down her sleeves inside her blue Chanel style jacket.

"It's good for your brain. Snaps you out of the blahs," Martha said, standing beside the car and facing Helen across the vehicle's low roof. Making some gyrations like she was massaging the air with her hands beside her ears, she said. "It gets the blood flowing."

"Straight to that one weak capillary in my head most likely to explode from a stroke induced from high amounts of gut-wrenching stress," Helen said as she walked toward the entrance to The Grange.

"You've been so crabby this morning," Martha said to Helen's back. "Try some deep breathing. It will relax you."

"Sure but riding with a sane driver would also be relaxing."

Martha shrugged. "But not as much fun. Right, buddy?"

No answer came from Helen as they rounded the corner path and walked under the portico of The Grange's main doors.

They always shuddered when they entered the old Elizabethan manor home, turned museum for rare books. Not more than two months ago, they'd stumbled onto a body in the reception area. Granted, it was the way they met and became good friends, but both girls, whenever they crossed The Grange's threshold, experienced a tinge of nervousness. It was the spot where they found their first body. Granted it was still alive at the time but they didn't know that.

Nevertheless, for the last two months, The Grange being also one of their clients, meant they'd been working on a project to assess its collection for conservation needs. There was a new curator in place, Aaron Blackwell, due to the fact that the last one had been murdered. Fresh from finishing his degree, he'd been hired by The Grange's governing board to bring some youthful energy to the "old pile" as Piers, the museum's board president, like to call it.

Once through the main entranceway, Helen and Martha moved down the dimly lit wainscoted hall to the library. They knew the route well, or thought they did.

"Mrs. Littleword?" asked an unexpected, loud male voice from a dark recess they didn't know existed in the paneling.

Helen and Martha screamed together in unison and jumped back against the far wall. Their nerves were always a trifle rough traveling down this hall due to their recent history of being stalked down its length by a crazed woman. Today was no exception.

A booming guffaw followed by a tall, young man in his late twenties, exploded out of the small recess. The new curator stood clutching his stomach in the hall laughing.

"Oh, that was a terrible thing to do. I'm so sorry but it was…" The attractive Mr. Aaron Blackwell was partially bent over giggling like a prankster teenager half his age.

"Mr. Blackwell," Helen, back straight with indignation, said hotly emphasizing each word in a staccato tone while staring at him like he was insane. "You have no idea how particularly frightening that was for Martha and I."

Martha put down her shoulder bag and said, "We clobbered the last person who sprung a surprise on us."

The young man's chortling slowly subsided as he caught the glint of steel in Martha's eyes.

"It was such a bad thing to do, but I had to because it was such a perfect opportunity. Mr. Cousins was showing me this tiny hallway built between the front and back parts of the house. It was used by the servants so they wouldn't be caught in the main part of the house. He thought it would be funny if…"

"Mr. Cousins?" Helen asked. "Piers are you back in there somewhere?" Helen pushed past Blackwell to find Piers smiling like a ten-year-old boy hiding behind the door.

"I can't believe you put him up to that, Piers," Helen said with fury in her eyes. She punched him brusquely on the shoulder. He winced but grinned impishly.

She pushed on. "You knew it would scare the daylight out of us but you did it anyway?"

"Yes and yes. Come here, Helen." He grabbed her clinched fist. "I saw you and Martha coming and something of the kid got into me."

His eyes never left Helen's. He pushed the door shut with Blackwell and Martha still standing on the other side and pulling Helen to him in the dark, he kissed her.

When Helen finally pulled back, her mind was reeling and before she was able to grasp onto a solid thought, Piers pulled her to him again and kissed her more intently, bending her neck toward his shoulder.

Blackwell knocked on the closed door and asked if they were okay. They pulled back from their embrace.

Helen tried to find the door knob, but Piers took her hand and guided her away from the door and back down the tight hallway in the opposite direction.

"Where are we going?" she asked still light-headed.

"We'll go around and meet them through the normal public way. I want to ask you something."

Helen didn't argue. She followed him feeling like a balloon tied to someone's wrist.

Piers pushed a door open. They found themselves in a sunlit room with boxes stored along a wall and old office machines cluttering the floor. But for the poster of a man holding some sort of government issued employment card advertising the proper screening of job applicants, Helen and Piers were alone. Piers turned to Helen and pulled her into his arms. He took one hand and tipped her face up to see into her eyes. She didn't resist. His beautiful blue eyes searched her face.

"You saved my life, Helen. On the bridge, the men were going to kill me and you never hesitated. What if you'd been hurt?" Piers shook his head. His hold on her tightened.

Helen wanted to get away from his embrace, the small room and the whole situation but at the same time she found his closeness intoxicating.

"Of course, I…" she wasn't sure what to say. Should she tell him her real feelings or say what was safe? Her mind wouldn't think straight so she offered, "I care about you, Piers. I would have done that for anybody I…" Fear clamped down on her causing the last word to stop in her throat.

"What Helen? Anybody you what?" Piers asked, trying to get her to finish her sentence.

"Care for." She let her tone carry the weight of her meaning.

The minute it was out of her mouth, she regretted it. She saw the sting in the tiny muscle spasm at the corner of his eyes and the change in his gaze. They went from soft to hurt in a blink of his lids. He relaxed his hold on her and stepped away.

"No, Helen. Your kiss said more."

Helen stood there with her arms dangling and her hands feeling like heavy dumbbells pulling downward to the floor. She was scared and unable to think straight. Too much had gone wrong in her life recently. Her husband's leaving only a year ago caused her to be extremely suspicious of getting involved in another relationship, especially with someone like Piers who had women fawning over him all the time. She didn't want to be hurt again and falling for Piers, if and when their relationship ended, would definitely hurt.

With all this flooding through her mind and the gulf between her and Piers widening by the moment, Helen eyes started to burn. With every fiber of her will, she told herself she absolutely would not cry.

Squaring her body to stare him straight in the eyes, Helen said, "Piers, I want you to listen to me."

Startled by her firmness, Piers peered down at her with a questioning gaze. She decided to be something she'd never been before in her life: extremely direct and honest with a man, even if it hurt him. If it backfired, fine, because she was tired of playing according to the rules of normal male-female interaction. Even her own ego was at play here. Her marriage had ended with her husband of twenty-five years running off with a girl half his age, so she'd try a different route this time.

"I won't be hurt again, Piers and I won't toy with you either. Your typical date is a runway model and I'm pretty sure I've got a weak spot in me wanting to prove I'm desirable just for ego's sake. You deserve better and I'm not interested in someone who sees me as a disposable commodity."

As she talked, her temper cooled and the stinging in her eyes melted away. She breathed easily. "I'm worth so much more than that and so are you."

Piers reached for her hand and she pushed it away.

"Piers, I would like us to be friends…for now. I want more time to try new things. Things I didn't take time for during the last thirty years. Do you understand?"

Piers nodded. The room was quiet. After a long pause, he said, "Friends, it is. I'm disappointed, though."

Helen laughed with relief and said, "You'll survive."

"You're an odd woman, Helen. Save me from the jaws of death to toss me out like yesterday's bathwater."

"Oh," she said in a soothing tone. "Don't be a drama king. I want you to come to a dinner party tonight to make up for last night. It's a party. It wouldn't be the same without the lord of the manor in attendance."

He laughed good-humoredly. "Well, in that case. I'll be there. Should I bring a date?"

Helen punched him in the ribs. "Do and I'll set Martha on you! Besides, I invited you, so be a gentleman, Piers."

“Women,” Piers said shaking his head.

“Indeed,” Helen answered.

They left the tight room full of old leftover, defunct machines and found their way around to the brightly lit entrance hall and into a new day.

CHAPTER 14

THAT SAME MORNING CHIEF JOHNS walked briskly into the Marsden-Lacey Constabulary and checked the duty roster. "Did Mrs. Littleword call in this morning to have an officer escort them to their work place? She was supposed to but I'm not holding my breath."

Sam Berry, the young cadet who was working on some paperwork answered. "No one called requesting an officer, Chief. Do you want someone to be on security detail today because I'm totally available."

Noting the young man's earnest desire to get away from the office and probably the ever-watchful eye of Donna, Johns scowled and thought for a moment. "Sam if you want to do something different today, go over to the soccer fields beside the canal and ask some of the kids if they saw anyone unusual hanging about yesterday. Don't do anything else. Take one of the police phones and call me if you find anything out. Okay?"

Total joy beamed from Sam's youthful face. "I'll be right on that, Sir."

"Do exactly what the Chief said, Sam, and nothing more. If you don't follow orders exactly, you won't have this kind of opportunity again for a long time. Do you understand?" Donna asked with the sternness of a military sergeant.

"I promise," the young man replied and then he was gone before anyone else forced him to comply with another rule.

Watching the teenager bounce out of the building, Chief Johns muttered to Donna, "I'll be in my office. Send Sergeant Endicott and Detective Richards in when you see them. We'll be out most of the morning. I am going over to Nottingham to talk with the forensic specialist on the case."

"Chief, a request has come in asking you to attend a Village Neighborhood Watch meeting tomorrow. Can you make it?" Donna called to his retreating back.

"No! I've got an investigation to work. I don't have time to tittle-tattle all evening with Grimsy and the ladies of Marsden-Lacy. Send Endicott. He's good with all that schmoozy stuff."

Johns ambled down the long hall to his new office grumbling the entire way. One thing good came out of being moved three doors down, he was closer to the washroom. After stopping in for a brief visit, he headed to his office.

Once settled at his desk, he leaned over and flipped the blinds up on the sunny windows. A steaming cup of black tea and the radiant heat from the sun made the room feel cozy and more familiar.

Opening the Laura Rossar-mescro file, he rifled through its contents until he found the document given to Helen from Stephan Rossar-mescro. It was in a mylar bag to keep it from being damaged. Studying the file and the document, he wondered if it would be possible to go on the internet and use a Russian-English translation application. But as he decided to give it a try, a heavy knock sounded at his door. Detective Richards from Nottingham and Sergeant Michael Endicott walked in.

"Ready to go, Johns?" Richards said with a big smile. "I'm counting on us eating at my favorite restaurant, Nandos."

"Oh yeah, they give a discount to the police don't they?" Michael said with a bright smile for the Chief.

"Do they?" Richards asked. "Doesn't matter though. I'd pay full price for that Peri-Peri chicken. It's that good."

Johns glanced back down at the file. "How about we eat at Nandos and run a copy of this over to the chap Helen Ryes mentioned." He searched for the name in his notes. "Thomas Albright. That's it. He'll be able to translate it."

"Sounds like a fun day. We've also got the appointment with Jinks at the forensic lab at eleven o'clock. Better get on the road," Richards said turning to go when Johns' phone rang.

"Yes," Johns said into the phone. "Okay. Sure, send him down. I'll talk with him."

Johns told Richards and Michael to bring a car around to the front. The men left and in a few minutes, there was a brisk tap at his door.

"Come in Mr. Turner," Johns called and the door swung open to reveal Alistair dapperly dressed and smiling.

"Mr. Turner, what can I do for you?"

Johns always found Perigrine and Alistair hard to read. Their dubious history was filled with unanswered questions regarding their involvement in possible criminal activities. He met them on a case in which they were mixed-up in a sting operation having to do with a group of counterfeiters. Somehow they managed to twist free of the major criminal counts, and got off serving a minimal sentence. Johns had a feeling there was always much more to the two men than what they appeared.

Alistair found a chair and sat down. “I’m here for two reasons. I read Russian and wanted to let you know that you have a thief problem at your house.”

Johns stiffened. His mind churning and red flags popping up. “Thief problem?”

“I think your Romani water travelers are parked along the Calder River somewhere below your farm and they’re messing about in your barns and are helping themselves to a few eggs. Mrs. Littleword ran into one this morning. Someone calling herself Miri.”

Red flags were forming themselves into flashing red warning signals in Johns’ mind. Miri was Stephan’s older sister. If the Romani people were camping on his farm, it was no longer a safe place for Martha and Helen or his mother. Whoever was hunting the Romani would be watching their movements. If Alistair was right, they would soon learn about the farm and see Helen. Johns’ instincts told him to act immediately. He needed to know Polly and the girls’ whereabouts.

“Did you leave my mother in the house, Alistair?” he asked.

Alistair shook his head. “Polly went down to the river to see where the water travelers were tied up.”

Shaking his head, Johns picked up his phone and dialed his mother’s number. No answer. Not a positive sign.

“Did you happen to hear where Helen and Martha went?” he asked while trying to dial Martha’s number.

"They left for The Grange. Something about work." Alistair sat up in his chair. "Do you want me to run over there and check on them?"

"No, but I do want you to try and remember exactly which direction you saw Mum walk. She's not answering her mobile, something she never does."

He dialed Martha's number. The phone call was only on its second ring when she answered.

"Hey, big guy." Martha's voice sounded cheerful. "What's up?"

A pleasant zing zipped through Johns when he heard her voice, but he didn't have the time to play phone-footsie with her. Instead, he asked, "Martha, are you and Helen somewhere fairly safe at the moment? You were supposed to call the constabulary when you left this morning and have an officer accompany you to work. I think it would be best if you both come immediately to the constabulary. I've been talking with Alistair Turner and he told me about the Romani woman, Miri, being at the farm this morning. If the Romani are being followed, the farm isn't safe anymore."

"We're wrapping up our work. It's about nine thirty now. I'll talk with Helen. I don't think she'll mind coming over." Then Martha said in a low whisper, "Probably have to bring Piers with us. He's being cozy with Helen this morning."

Johns got an idea. "Martha, is Piers close by or will you please have him call me immediately?"

Martha said she would have him call, but her tone told him there was a lack of enthusiasm for the request. He knew Martha didn't like to be managed. As a few minutes passed, Johns and Alistair waited tensely without much conversation. Finally the phone rang.

"That you, Cousins?" Johns asked without even a hello into the receiver.

"Yes, Chief. What do you need?"

"Would you do me a big favor and take the girls to Healy for the rest of the day? I need them somewhere safe. They'd probably prefer being there than tucked into a jail cell here at the constabulary. Flower Pot Cottage isn't safe and neither is the farm until I get some men over there."

"Absolutely," Piers said.

Johns was beginning to think better of Cousins. He was proving to be a good sort after all.

"Thank you, Cousins. I'll keep in touch. One thing more, I know the Calder runs through your estate. If you wouldn't mind having your gamekeeper check to see if there are any canal boats tethered anywhere along your banks, I would appreciate it. Boat numbers, colors and flags would be extremely helpful." The Chief hung up the phone. Alistair's expression was grim.

"Something on your mind, Mr. Turner?"

Johns detected the muscles of Alistair's jaws twitching, but otherwise the man was unreadable.

"I would like to give you some advice, Chief, that is if you'll have it?" Alistair said.

"Appreciate anything you're willing to share, Mr. Turner," Johns said with genuine interest. He knew Alistair was unsure, or perhaps unwilling, to say everything on his mind, so he waited.

"I would offer that you might be careful who you choose to translate the document the gypsy man gave you. I think there may be some unscrupulous or more likely, dangerous people, who'd like to get their hands on it."

Johns regarded Turner intensely for a brief moment. "Why do you think this?"

"You've got a Russian letter, two murders in as many towns and three gypsy boats with unusual house flags. Those flags have a black eagle on them and if I'm not mistaken it's an imperial eagle."

"Meaning a Russian heritage perhaps?" Johns asked.

Alistair shook his head, "Meaning those Romani have something that's caught the attention of a person who hires eastern European hit men."

"How did you learn this?"

"Helen Ryes told us at breakfast. Piers Cousins heard the men's accents when they were going to kill him on the bridge, but I guess you probably already know this."

"Yes, and I've got a colleague in ACRO who is checking on known criminals fitting the descriptions Cousins gave us last night. We're focusing on illegals from eastern Europe and of course Russia. The background checks on the Romani family have come back clean. They've got a nice English pedigree going back a few generations."

"Let me come with you to search for Polly," Alistair said. "I would like to talk with the Rossar-mescros and Perigrine will be useful as well."

"Thank you, but I don't want to involve either of you in something potentially dangerous. I'm going to try my mother one more time and if she doesn't answer, I will take another constable with me to find her. In the meantime, Mr. Turner, if you should come across any information regarding the men we are seeking, I would greatly appreciate a head's up."

Alistair glanced down at the file still open on Johns' desk with the infamous document lying on top.

"I'm taking this to a man Helen Ryes suggested in Nottingham. He may be able to translate it. He's retired from a branch of the government that dealt with translations. It probably holds the key to this entire investigation," Johns said, never taking his eyes off Alistair.

The debonair, well-dressed man's face never hinted at his inner thoughts. All he said was, "Whoever you show it to, will most likely need serious police protection. Not everyone who's worked for the government is of the highest moral fiber."

Johns considered his point. He stood up and walked over to the corner table where the hot water maker sat and flipped the button at its base causing the water to begin to boil and hiss. "That's a copy. The real letter is in London for carbon dating and DNA testing."

He turned to Alistair who was now standing in the doorway and said, "If this man can't help us, I would appreciate your assistance. I don't want to endanger your life Mr. Turner…yet."

Alistair laughed good-humoredly at the Chief's remark. "How dull for us. The offer is there if you need it. Thank you for your concern."

As Johns watched, Alistair disappeared around the doorframe into the hallway and the phone rang again on his desk. Reaching over, he grabbed the receiver.

"Yes?" he said. "Thank God, Mum. Where are you?" Listening, he said in a serious tone, "I'll be right there."

Johns hung up the phone and hurried out of his office to where Endicott and Richards were waiting for him in the parking area. He jumped into the car.

"Boys, we're going to need to change vehicles. We'll need the Land Rover for where we're going."

"Aren't we going to Nottingham?" Richards asked, sounding disappointed and laying a protective hand on his comfortable paunch.

"No, we're going to collect my mother whose bullheadedness has nearly got her killed. Call Jinx at the forensic lab and tell her we'll be there later. Come on!"

In less than five minutes, the ten men pulled out of the yard driving a military, green colored utility vehicle. A light drizzle was falling, causing Johns to curse loudly about the English weather and drive even faster toward his family farm. He prayed he'd get there in time.

CHAPTER 15

THE RAIN WAS FALLING IN sheets around the car making Martha's ability to see the road difficult. She was following Helen and Piers to Healy but remembering her pets at the farm, she slipped down a different road, making a slight detour to check on them.

Ditches were collecting rainwater and cast-off leaves along the narrow country lane. The temperature was dropping from the cold front moving in. Martha turned up the heat in the Mini Cooper as she worried about her pets huddled in the barn, probably distraught from the storm. With the wipers whipping back and forth across the windshield and the rain lashing the car, she was barely able to make out the beautiful timbered barns in the distance indicating she was getting closer to Johns' farm.

Pulling in through the gate and slowly driving the tight road to the house, an uneasy feeling crept upon her. She reached for her purse and dug around inside for her cell phone looking at the time. It was still early, only a little after ten o'clock. Once she made it to the front of the old farm house, she saw Polly's car still in the same place it had been earlier that morning. It was tucked into one of the old stalls of the front shed. Martha stopped the Mini Cooper and turned off the engine. As sudden blast of wind buffeted the car and whipped the rain with ferocity causing her to hesitate about going out into the storm.

A final thought for personal safety caused her to pick up her cell phone. She sent a message to Helen saying she'd made a quick stop at Polly's to check on her pets and would be on her way to Healy in a few minutes. Throwing the car door open, she jumped out and ran toward the barn hopping over puddles and dodging small, muddy rivulets of water. She pushed hard on the big door, forcing it to swing open applying her entire weight upon it to shut it once again. There were no lights on in the old building making it dark and difficult to see in. Amos came rushing up with a cheerful greeting and a wagging tail.

"How are you, Fuzzy Pants," Martha cooed lovingly to the furry four-pounder. "You are getting around so much better today." Soon loud, distraught mewing came from the horse stall. Gus and Vera squeezed through the stall gate and came trotting over to Martha with their tails high in the air. They rubbed their sides along her legs mewing to be picked up.

"Well, aren't you two being extremely affectionate?"

She reached down to collect both cats which wasn't particularly easy because Gus was topping twelve pounds the last time he went to the vet. The vexed felines cried and complained about their harsh living accommodations while Amos sat smiling and wagging her tail so that it brushed the barn's hay strewn floor collecting straw in the few inches of long wiry fur remaining on the tip of her tail.

"Come on, kids, I'm taking you with me. This has all been too much for you. Let's get you in your carriers and into the car. I shouldn't have brought you here. You would be much happier at Lillian's."

Whenever Martha would go out of town, she would often have a friend named Lillian babysit her menagerie. Stuffing the cats into one carrier and Amos into another, she comfortably tucked them into their tiny, portable dens. They became quiet and docile. Peeking in to see their faces, she knew by the cats' expressions they might hold a grudge for a while.

Headed for the door of the barn with a carrier under each arm, she stopped dead in her tracks. Coming along the side of the building, she heard men's voices speaking in an accent that sounded Russian. It immediately dawned on her, these could be the same men who attacked Piers or were skulking around her cottage.

If she went outside, they would run right into them. Quickly scanning the barn, Martha saw a huge pile of hay against the far wall. With no time to waste in case they should come inside the barn, she ran over and quietly burrowed into the straw, covering herself and the two pet carriers. She whispered to the cats and Amos to stay quiet.

Soon, the barn door's hinges creaked, telling her she'd been right about them possibly coming inside. Amos growled in a low guttural way and Martha hushed her. Studying Martha sideways, Amos' eyes questioned whether this approach was a sound one, but with dutiful compliance, she laid her head down between her paws in quiet submission.

The men were staying in one place. They must be waiting out the storm thought Martha. As if on cue, the wind died back. She heard car doors slam outside and the two men chattered nervously between themselves in the same Russian language.

Martha hesitated about what to do. Who might be outside? Would the men decide to hide, too? What if they picked the same haystack she was in? It was in the middle of her worried musings that an answer supplied itself. Martha heard a scratching noise and a soft rustling against her back. Her mind flashed "mouse" and she levitated out of the hay like someone had set fire to her back end.

"Ahhhh!" Martha screamed, bounding free from her hay-mound tomb.

The men jumped at the sound of her scream and turned around in time to see a crazed, straw-encrusted banshee flying at them. Turning frantically, they pulled on the door of the barn to escape, but as they got it open they came face to face with Johns, Detective Richards and Sergeant Endicott.

Scene Break

SURPRISE BLANCHED THE FACES OF all five men, but it was Sergeant Endicott and Richards who gave chase to the men as they ran out into the open pasture. Johns stayed put and watched them go.

Besides, with a green Mini Cooper parked not more than twenty feet away and the sound of that all too familiar scream, he wanted to get a better look at what put such fear into those two men that they were willing to take their chances outside in the storm instead of staying dry in the barn.

Johns poked his head through the door and everything went black. He woke up lying on his back with the subtle perfume of gardenias mixing with a pounding pain in his head. As he willed the barn roof to come into focus, a face slowly moved into his peripheral vision. It was like watching a sunrise. First, it rose from the horizon line and with its looming intensity so close, he shut his eyes to block-out the sheer magnitude and nearness of the orb.

"Are you alright?" Martha whispered into his ear.

He realized the perfume must be hers. Opening his eyes, he found himself staring into a dense mass of red hair riddled with straw pieces sticking out of it in every direction. A light pressure on his chest told him she had her head laying there.

"What are you doing?" he asked in a soft voice.

Her head popped up off his chest and again the orb loomed right next to his face causing him to blink.

"Checking to see if you were still alive," she said, keeping her voice a whisper.

"You haven't killed me yet. You're doing a great job of trying. I'll give you that, but I'm fortunately made of fairly hardy stock." He winced as he tried to sit up.

Martha helped him into an upright position. "I thought you were one of the men coming back."

Johns' stomach took a nose dive. Like a man ready to kill someone with his own two hands, he took in her disheveled hair with pieces of hay mashed into it and his mind skyrocketed to a horrible place.

"Did they touch you?" he demanded. "I'll kill them." He tried to get to his feet.

Martha pulled him back down to earth with a firm tug on his arm. "Absolutely not, sweetie. They never knew I was in the barn." She patted his arm. "I didn't know it was *your* head I… well… tapped, until you were lying on the ground."

"Tapped? You call that a tap?" He rubbed the protruding knot on the back of his cranium. "Woman, why are you so damned difficult?"

Martha smiled up at him sweetly and leaned in closely putting her index finger on his lips as a sign he should shut up. "You're cute when you're mad. Are you done fussing about that smidgen of a bump?"

Johns had never in his life been talked to by a woman like that, but he kind of liked it. Her closeness made his heart beat faster and the smell of her perfume filled his head like a drug. Martha gazed steadily into his eyes and smiled as she leaned in. He knew what was coming so he shut his eyes and… a light kiss nipped the tip of his nose.

"All better?" she asked.

His eyelids flung open and feeling stupid and terribly disappointed, he peered into her mischievous face. He reached out and with his heart thumping, he pulled her deep into his embrace and kissed her for a long time.

Martha didn't pull away. She let him hold her. They stayed that way until footsteps and voices came back over the pasture. Jumping up, they dusted themselves off and Johns helped Martha pull straw out of her red, curly hair.

Once they knew Richards and Michael were only a few feet from the barn, Johns went outside to talk with the two men and Martha collected her crated pets still buried in the hay.

"What happened to you?" Detective Richards asked Johns when he got close enough to see the Chief.

"Mrs. Littleword whacked me on the head thinking I was one of the men you gave chase to across the field. Any luck?"

"No. They made it into the woods over there." Michael pointed to the tree line in the distance. The two men were soaked to the bone.

"Come on, let's get indoors," Johns said. "Mum's probably got a fire going. Dry you both out and then we need to get off to Nottingham."

Johns banged on the old oak door to his home and yelled, "Mum, it's me. Let us in! It's all clear!"

Soon they heard the grating of metal on metal and the door swung open to reveal Polly holding a shotgun and wearing a holster with an old pistol from the early twentieth century.

"Loaded for bear?" Martha asked Polly casually as she walked past carrying her crated pets and followed by the three men all glancing nervously at the grey-haired woman wielding the firearms.

"Damn right! It's about time you got here, Merriam. I've been pacing this place half out of my mind."

Johns knew his mother would have enjoyed shooting anyone who broke into her home, but she was getting on in years and he didn't want her to hurt herself trying to kill an intruder. Plus, it was against the law to have any weapon you intend to use to hurt another person. He needed to discreetly retrieve the firearms after she cooled off.

"They're gone, Mum, but I don't want you staying here tonight. I have you, Mrs. Littleword and Mrs. Ryes nice accommodations over at Healy House."

Polly slammed her shotgun down on the long, oak table, giving everyone in the room a jolt. With a steely stare she said, "If you think I'm leaving my brewery and chickens so that half the country can lay their thieving hands on my stock and drink my beer, you've got another think coming."

"Your mother is right. We aren't running. Better to stay here and shoot anyone who comes near. Sends the right kind of message," Martha said munching on one of the breakfast biscuits leftover from breakfast. "Do you have any jam, Polly? I'm starving."

Polly's expression as she handed Martha the jam pot spoke volumes. "You're my kind of person, Littleword. I think you and I can get on just fine." Turning to her son, she said, "Merriam, I'm staying here tonight and so is Mrs. Littleword. If Mrs. Ryes would like to stay, she's welcome, too."

Martha swallowed the contents of her mouth and said, "Polly, call me Martha."

Polly nodded assertively and announced to the assemblage. "Martha, and I will be staying here tonight. No arguments."

Johns knew when it would take an act of God to change his mother's mind so he sighed resignedly and told Sergeant Endicott and Detective Richards to thaw out in front of the lovely old inglenook fireplace where a friendly fire crackled and popped.

After the men were settled with warm cups of tea, Johns returned to the reason they were here in the first place.

"Mum, what did you see down by the river?" he asked.

She inhaled and let out a big sigh. "Three narrowboats nestled against the embankment on our side of the river. It was the Romani people. They didn't see me. It was when I was coming back to the farm I saw the other two men snooping about the barns. I was quick and stayed low letting myself in through the back. Got the doors all locked, loaded the shotgun and found your grandfather's old military pistol and waited for you to get here."

"I'm glad you're safe. You did the right thing by calling and not shooting them yourself. Detective Richards and I will pay a visit to our water traveler friends. I'll let them know the eggs were a gift, but no more helping themselves to our provisions. Are you sure you still want to have your dinner party here tonight?"

"Absolutely, I do. Should be starting about 7:00 o'clock. Please be back in time Merriam."

"I'll try, but I think I'll leave Sergeant Endicott with you. I'll feel better if someone stays here for protection."

"That's fine, better to hold down the fort," Polly said with keenness in her expression. "Never know what might crawl out and come knocking about."

"Have it your way, but stay close to the house and don't leave unless you take precautions," Johns said.

He left his mother and Martha chatting and laughing happily about the time Martha shot her brother "accidentally" with a pellet gun.

"Michael, I'm leaving you here. Get comfortable and I'll have my mother bring you some of my clothes to change into. She won't budge from this house so I need to know she is safe."

He saw the disappointment on the young Sergeants' face. "I'll make sure to bring you some Peri-Peri chicken from Nandos. Come on Richards, let's get to Nottingham, but before we go, we're going to check-in on the Rossar-mescro family down below the farm. They've made themselves comfortable on the Calder. Shouldn't take us long to drive there."

Though it wasn't the time or the place to talk any further with Martha, he still wanted to be alone with her one more time before he left. Their kiss was difficult to forget. He knew by the conversation the two women were having, she'd won Polly over. Not an easy task for him most days, but Martha being who she was would easily charm his mother. He tried to catch her eye and when that didn't work, he said, "Mrs. Littleword, would you like some help putting your car in the barn?"

Martha smiled, "Actually I would like to take my pets to a friend in the village. Her name is Lillian Cadmen. They'll be happier there. They're used to being indoors and sleeping with someone."

"Bring them indoors," Polly said with a wave of her hand indicating she didn't mind. "I've had everything living in this house at some point or other. Dogs, cats, a rabbit named Ernest, two parakeets and my favorite, a wee pig, answering to the name of Cuddles. The pig was the cleanest and the smartest of all, including the humans I've housed."

"Gus and Vera will probably be better off at Lillian's because of your chickens, but I'd like to keep Amos close by while she's getting over her injuries. She's a good dog," Martha said. "I'll call Lillian and drop them off on the way through the village on my way to Healy."

"Why don't you stay here?" Polly asked. "Call Helen and have her come over here. We'll have fun cooking together."

"That's not a bad idea. We could go together to the village and pick up what we need for the dinner. I'll call Helen and tell her to come back. With Sergeant Endicott here, we are in safe hands."

"Be careful," Johns said. "You take Endicott where ever you go."

"We will. I'm taking the gun," Polly said.

"No, you're not."

Johns turned to Sergeant Endicott. "If they leave, go with them. Hide the guns. Mum may try and use them. Not a good idea."

Johns and Detective Richards left the house to head down to the Calder for a conversation with the Romani while Polly and Martha created a shopping list. Polly didn't believe in canceling a dinner party because of a slight threat of skulking Russian hit-men. With a disgruntled Endicott in tow, they were off to deliver the cats then to the market to buy ingredients for jambalaya and hushpuppies. The evening festivities were shaping up to be spicy and possibly a bit hot to handle.

CHAPTER 16

TUCKED UP IN A SUNNY room strewn with toys from multiple generations of Cousins and covered in a faded, toile wallpaper portraying frolicking animals from nursery rhymes and fairy tales, Emerson sat playing on an up-to-date toy, a Nintendo DS. He was trying desperately to defeat a troll and make it to the next level of the game.

A knock on the door and a cheerful greeting announced Celine's arrival with the wonderful lunch tray heaped with fancy treats and sandwiches from Senior Agosto's confectionary repertoire.

The child, delighted, scrambled off his daybed and bounced across the room to the diminutive table and chairs that served as the nursery's dining facilities. Celine reminded him about washing his hands and with only a small grumble, he complied.

"I think I've almost made it to the eighth level, Celine," Emerson said as he sat down to begin munching on a delicate sandwich of cucumbers and cream cheese already prepared for him on his plate.

"Even though it's your free day, you'd better not be ignoring your Latin homework, Emmy?" Celine said with an eyebrow slightly arched to show she would know if he tried to fudge on the answer.

"Oh, it's so boring! If I lived like Tallant on one of the boats down in the river, I wouldn't need to know stupid Latin."

Emerson reached for another sandwich.

Celine tapped his outstretched hand and pointed to his napkin. “You need to wipe the corners of your mouth and politely ask if you may have another sandwich.”

Emerson pursed his lips and sighed. Constant attention to his manners took all the fun out of life and only increased his desire to be free and live like the gypsy boy, Tallant.

“Besides,” Celine said, “you need to tell me who this Tallant person is before you start on another sandwich.”

“He’s my friend. I met him out by the garden where Senior Agosto keeps his plants. We built a fort in one of the big trees down by the place where Mr. Chattersworth is making his fox trap. Tallant doesn’t like the idea of us catching the fox. He says it should be free to be what God made him to be.”

Celine studied the child and laid another sandwich on his plate receiving a grin from him for her good deed.

“Emmy, I would like to meet Tallant before you play again and I think Mr. Cousins would be interested as well in your new playmate. Why don’t you invite him to the nursery for tea? We’ll make a special time of it. No more playing down by the water or so far away from the house until I’ve met him. Okay?”

The child shrugged and said, “Sure, Celine.”

Thinking about the “special time of it,” he gave her a big smile and begged, “Can we have crisps and a lemon cake if he comes?”

The nanny laughed, knowing she would not begrudge him his childish whim. “Yes. A lemon cake, crisps and maybe ice cream. What a nutritious meal. But only if you do as I say, and bring Tallant to meet me and your Uncle Piers."

"It's a deal," Emerson said offering his small hand for Celine to seal the arrangement. The two diners, nanny and ward, gave each other a firm handshake and continued to enjoy their cozy tea as the sky outside took on billowy clouds and rain tapped gently on the nursery windows. They paid it no attention for the storm was no competition for the lightness and tastiness of a Senior Agosto custard tart topped with world finest Cornish clotted cream.

CHAPTER 17

SAM BERRY SAT MISERABLY HUNCHED over in the drizzling rain trying to remember why he'd ever been interested in Penny Cartwright in the first place. For at least a year, he thought she was the woman of his dreams, but she was making his life difficult with her constant texting and hints at marriage.

Since Sam's personal makeover, both physical and career-wise, Penny was pushing him to settle down. He was only eighteen and for a while it was great, but recently he'd seen Piers Cousins' new housekeeper, Celine Rupert, and thoughts of Penny were pushed out the door like yesterday's dust bunnies.

Celine was above and beyond his wildest dreams of a woman. Beautiful, long blonde hair almost the color of cream, she must have been a ballet dancer the way she held herself and practically floated across the floor.

He'd seen her one day when Chief Johns asked him to take papers out to Healy House to give to Mr. Cousins. Celine answered the door. Sam found it difficult to find his tongue, dislodge it from the roof of his mouth, and hand over the papers to her. He would never forget how she smiled at him and said, "Thank you. I'll see he gets these."

Her voice was melodious. Like a ray of glorious sunshine, she floated back inside and was gone as the door solidly shut in his mooning face. He had been able to think about nothing else and Penny's pestering was extremely irksome with this new love in his life.

As the rain pattered on his umbrella, Sam checked his watch. It was almost lunchtime. His stomach was always hungry and his Aunt Harriet's mince pies were some of the best made in the village. With visions of meat pies filling his head, he wished the soccer players would wrap up their game and come over to collect their things.

Finally, three young boys in their mid teens ran over to wipe off their faces and drink from their water bottles. Sam recognized them to be from his school but a few years behind him. He walked over and they nodded an acknowledgement.

"Hey, it's a copper. What you doin' Berry? Playing Cops and Robbers?" one boy gibed. Sam knew his name was Jeremy. The rest of the boys laughed and gawked at the police recruit.

"Yeah, Sam, what happened to your hair? I didn't recognize you with just your face," another pimple-faced boy said.

Sam, unperturbed by what he believed were the humorless comments of youngsters, affected a bored expression. "You seen anybody hanging around here lately that looks smarter than you muppets?"

The boys scowled at Sam's sarcasm and thought for a moment. It was Jeremy who spoke up first.

"Nah. I haven't seen anyone."

"So many people use the tow paths to get about," the boy with the acne said.

“Let me know if you see any rough types coming or going, would you? Stay away from them. They’re trouble,” Sam said.

The boys exchanged sullen but wary glances and ran off to finish their game in the mud and water-soaked field. They yelled a few more taunts back at Sam who good-naturedly shook his head and wondered at what was becoming of today’s youth.

CHAPTER 18

"WHAT ARE YOU STUDYING, ALISTAIR?" Perigrine asked, coming through the back door to their office carrying his shopping from Murdock's Grocery. Filled with things for tonight's dinner at Polly's, the bags made a heavy clunking sound once settled on the kitchen counter. Perigrine began to pull out the different items and put them away.

Finished, he gave Alistair another opportunity to answer but nothing came. Finally, though still intently studying his laptop's screen, Alistair gave a half-hearted hello to Perigrine's earlier entrance.

The storm brewing all morning was picking up energy. Rain fell in torrents accompanied by another loud round of thunder grumbling over the village trying to rattle windows and fiddle with the nerves of the good inhabitants of Marsden-Lacey.

Perigrine, not typically bothered by a stormy day, was feeling unusually edgy and discontented. All morning, after their visit to Johns' farm, a restless feeling that things were building to a head plagued him. His mind searched for what it was as he finished putting away groceries, but the exact location of his uneasiness eluded him.

"Alistair?" he asked, raising his voice to dispel the shadowy thoughts lurking in the crevices of his consciousness and to rouse Al from his deep investigation of the internet.

"Something tells me you've been productive at the constabulary. How did your conversation with the Chief go?"

With a quick swivel of his office chair so he was facing Perigrine dead on, Alistair's face expressed a suppressed excitement.

"What is it?" Perigrine asked. His irritation with Alistair's muteness was growing each silent second.

"Those boats…if I'm right, P., may hold the key to one of the greatest treasure finds of the twenty-first century. Unfortunately, I think we've some rough competition for the bag."

Holding a can of dog food half-way between heaven and the table below, Perigrine's face registered his lack of understanding. "What boats are you talking about?"

"The gypsy boats."

Alistair took a deep breath and slowly let it out. P.'s brain ran over the last few days' accumulated events. All morning, his intuition told him something was about to burst over Marsden-Lacey. Things were beginning to fall into place. Sitting down in his favorite Bergere chair, he asked, "What's on the internet you're so engrossed in?"

"That, my friend, is how I know it's something to do with the boats. It's the letter the Rossar-mescros brought to Helen Ryes. The author was an Imperial Guard of the Russian royal family, or the late Romanovs."

Alistair swirled back around to face the computer screen. "From what I can tell by reading it, he had four items belonging to Her Imperial Majesty, the Dowager Empress Maria Feodorovna, which he wished to see her sister, Her Majesty Queen Alexandra, accept and hold until they were returned to the Dowager Empress." Alistair stopped and thought for a moment.

"The list at the bottom is also in Russian and that's where it gets interesting. They are: Empire, Blue Hen, Cherub, Mauve. Ring any bells?" Alistair asked with a huge smile from ear to ear.

Perigrine thought for a moment. Like a glorious dawn, the light filtered in to those places in his mind where dark thoughts had flickered all day. "But there are only three boats. Which one is missing?"

"Mauve," Alistair answered. Taking a deep breath, he turned to Perigrine. "I think it was too incredible for either of us to actually let our minds go there and besides, the names are so indistinct, but they match up perfectly."

Alistair's enthusiasm was growing on Perigrine. The fabulous truth was dawning on him as well. Normally, he liked to stay grounded emotionally, but it was like someone was blowing up a balloon in his stomach and, like it or not, he was beginning to become buoyant.

"Oh my God! Alistair, do you think they're on those boats?"

"That's the tricky part. Maybe and maybe not, but one thing's for sure, we aren't the only people who are onto the same idea. What did you think when Helen mentioned Albright's name and then Johns going to see him?"

Perigrine's mouth tightened into a grim, thin line. "That was a shock. I thought Tom had gone underground, but when Helen Ryes said she knew someone in Nottingham who worked on translations, it isn't any doubt that's him. He's not someone I want to know about our whereabouts."

"Well," Alistair continued with Perigrine's thoughts, "that means we have to move fast. Do you think Helen Ryes is who she says she is?"

"It's hard to tell. Albright is a dirty deal if there ever was one. Have you checked her out, yet?"

Alistair plunked around on his computer key board. "She seems squeaky clean, but if she's ever been one of Albright's people, then she'd be like your sister; hard to find in legal records."

Perigrine raised his gaze to the ceiling as if the answer for the questionable enigma of his sister resided somewhere up in the rafters. "How fast do we need to move and when?"

"Very fast. Tonight perhaps. Sound feasible?"

"I like it. Let's get it together," Alistair said with a grin.

Perigrine studied the document photos on Alistair's laptop screen. "How did you get these photos? Did Johns give it to you?"

"No. I snapped it with my phone when he turned his back to make tea. Modern technology can be so convenient."

"Al, do you think we might really find those eggs?" Perigrine asked.

"Well," chuckled Alistair as he swiveled around in his chair to smile rakishly at Perigrine, "that, my dear old friend, is the million dollar question or should I say the millions and millions of dollars question."

CHAPTER 19

THE POLICE UTILITY VEHICLE'S WINDSHIELD wipers flipped back and forth trying to cope with the deluge of rain falling from the dark, cloud filled sky. Johns and Detective Richards bumped down the muddy, root-tangled road, and over an open space of pasture till they reached the spot where the water travelers were tied up. A couple of men were working on the embankment cutting up wood and tossing it to another man on deck who stacked the pieces.

"How do you suppose these people make a living?" Richards asked as Johns slowed the vehicle and put the hand brake on once they were completely stopped.

"That's a good question. There isn't much work anymore for cargo along these canals like there was seventy years ago, but some people do odd jobs, make jewelry to sell, or it's possible they're on the dole."

Johns twisted to see in the back and pulled out two pairs of Wellington boots. "Here. You're going to need these."

They put on the rain gear and headed off down the slope to the place where the men were working. As they came across the stile, one of the men saw them and waved. Johns recognized Stephan Rossar-mescro and returned the greeting. Stephan walked down the bank away from the boats to meet them. The other family members went about their work and only occasionally glanced over to where the three men talked.

"I see you've moved up the river, Stephan," Johns said.

"Yes, we won't go back to the other place. It's better for us in the countryside. Do you know who killed Laura?" Stephan asked.

"Mr. Rossar-mescro, there are dangerous men tracking your family. In fact, I know they've found you here. They're either eastern Europeans or Russians. Is there anything you may be involved in that you haven't told me?"

Fear drained the older man's face of all color. "What can I do to protect my family? What do they want?"

Johns hoped for this reaction. "Stephan, I'd like to put your boats under police protection by bringing them back to Marsden-Lacey. We'll take your family to a safe house until we catch these men. I've requested additional men from our Nottingham Headquarters and from Interpol. It should only be a matter of time until we catch the killer or killers."

Stephan shook his head. "I don't know. The Rossar-mescros haven't left their boats in over ninety years. They're our only home. Would we be safe back in our home waters below London?"

"No," Johns said adamantly. "These men want something which brings me back to the document you gave Helen Ryes. Who else has seen the letter besides your family?"

"Like I said earlier, it was Laura who handled the business with the letter. I'm frightened for my family. Since

Laura's death we've been followed. Yesterday, a dark headed man with sunglasses watched us from the wood over there. Miri said it was the hunter, but I shot at him and he fled so it was no more ghost than you or me."

"Stephan, you know it's against the law to shoot at anyone. I'll need to see your gun permits. I don't want you getting into trouble by letting your fear take over."

Mr. Rossar-mescro hung his head. "It's my duty to protect my family. I've already failed once."

"You are the father to your people, so I can offer you safety, but you need to turn those boats around at the bend up the river and head back to the village," Johns said.

"Okay. We will leave in an hour. This will take us some time, but I think we can be in Marsden-Lacey by nightfall."

Johns thanked him for helping the investigation in this way and the two policemen climbed the embankment and got in the police vehicle.

"That's a relief," Johns said as he started the engine. "If we lost another one, someone from Headquarters would be climbing down my throat."

"You did the right thing. Getting them away from those boats will stop the killings," Richards said.

Johns nodded. "Let's get back to the constabulary and change cars. I need to call Albright to make sure he'll meet with us today. Helen Ryes knows him. She'll have his number."

CHAPTER 20

"YES, CHIEF I WILL SEND it to you. I haven't seen Thomas in about three years, but I know he still takes odd jobs. Good luck and please let me know what you find out." Helen tapped the glass screen to end the call.

"What's going on?" Piers asked. He was holding the door open for Helen to get into his Jaguar. She was trying to hurry and get in before the rain completely soaked her to the skin. They had finished a light lunch at Healy when Helen received a call from the Chief filling her in on the situation at the farm.

"I'm sending a contact to Chief Johns. He needs the name of a gentleman in Nottingham who used to work for the Government Communications Headquarters. Hopefully, Mr. Albright will be able to help us translate the letter. By the way, Martha never made it here because she's been in a bit of a rough and tumble over at Johns' farm."

"Is she okay?" Piers asked.

"She's fine, but she and Polly want to stay at the farm. They've got Sergeant Endicott with them and want me to come back over there. Are we ready to go?"

Piers and Helen were sitting in the warm car with the heater blowing and the wipers working to beat off the heavy rain. Coming around the side of the house they saw Mr. Chattersworth, the gamekeeper, walking toward them.

"I'd better see what Chattersworth wants. I can tell he's got something to tell me. I'll be right back." Piers got out and quickly flipped open an umbrella then tried to hurry and meet the older man.

"Hello, Mr. Chattersworth. Any luck seeing boats down on our embankments?"

The older gentleman dressed in a knee-length rain jacket, big-brimmed hat and water-proof boots was carrying a bee smoker in one hand. He hurried to Piers with his head down to keep his face from being pelted by the rain.

"Mr. Cousins, Sir, I've been to the bee yard and I think they may be ready to start quieting down for the season. We won't be taking anymore honey till next spring but Senior Agosto is fit to be tied and feels I've shortened the season. That bull-headed Spaniard is threatening to cut me off on my food rations. You've got to talk with him, Mr. Cousins. I won't be harassed about me bees."

Piers waved his hand in the air in a gesture to diffuse the domestic riff often caused by Agosto's hot temper. "I'll talk with him, Chattersworth, but do tell me what you saw on the river?"

The older man pulled on the brim of his rain hat. He struck a pose that older men will do when about to digress into a much longer story than most younger men want to hear. Piers, being in a hurry but not wanting to offend his faithful gamekeeper, inwardly took a silent pause and waited politely for the long-winded answer yet to come.

"I was down by the old oak trees near the lower field where we've set the fox trap and I see this youngster messing about the place and I say to him, 'What are you doing here, child?' and he stares me down like I've stole his tongue. I say again, 'This is a private piece of ground and you need to state your business.'"

Chattersworth nodded at Piers as if that answered the original question completely. Piers, unsure, wondered if it was time to delicately discuss retirement with Chattersworth, but as he was ticking that idea into his mental calendar of events, the gamekeeper caught his breath and continued.

"The child stood tall and said to me, 'You shouldn't be killing foxes and trapping them. They're born to do their work like you and me.' Well, that's when I said, 'And my work, young man, is to see to it that those foxes don't take another of my chickens.'"

Again, Chattersworth nodded and pursed his mouth in such a way as to indicate the trials he dealt with daily. Piers waited, giving it time and soon his patience was rewarded.

"I asked the child where he hailed from and he says as nice as you please that his name is Tallant and he was living with his family downstream on the Empire. I told him I'd leave him to manage foxes as he pleased in his Empire and I'd manage mine the way it pleases Mr. Cousins in his. Haven't seen him since, but the fox trap was fiddled with and that means I've got to go down there, after I put the bees to sleep, and put it back together."

Piers sighed inwardly and hoped the diatribe was finished. He dared to ask the question one last time hoping to get a firm yes or no for an answer. "So, no boats on our embankments, right?"

"Not a one, Mr. Cousins, and if I see one I'll let you know," Chattersworth said with a big compliant smile.

"Thank you, and as always, you do such good work for us and for Healy, Mr. Chattersworth. Sometime soon we might have a talk…over tea."

Piers backed toward the car and waved to the man who was already walking briskly down to the bee yard.

Opening the driver's side door, Piers sat down.

"Are we leaving?" Helen asked.

Piers sat with his hands on the steering wheel thinking about what Chattersworth said. "Helen, do you mind if I run upstairs for a moment? I want to check on something with Emerson and Celine."

"Absolutely. I'm fine waiting. Take your time. I've some emails to answer."

"Great. I'll be right back."

Piers again jumped out of the car and into the storm. He ran up the steps to the front door and shot up the inside stairwell, down a long corridor and up another flight till he was standing in front of the nursery door.

"Is that you, Uncle Piers?" a small voice said from inside. The old mahogany door creaked as it slowly swung open to only a small crack. One round blue eye at about elbow level gazed at him. The game was on, so Piers puffed up in a playful gorilla posture and said, "I'm going to get you!"

The child squealed and ran from the door as Piers stomped into the nursery to see Celine smiling at the fun and Emerson running to the far corner of the room to hide inside the closet.

Piers put his index finger over his lips to indicate to Celine to stay quiet as he approached the door with each of his feet coming down hard on the carpet like a giant. With each thump of his foot, the child in the closet let out a happy screech until Piers swung the door open to be mauled by a springing Emerson.

The man tossed the boy into the air. Tucking him under one paternal arm, he hauled him across the room laughing till he plopped him down on the daybed. This game had begun only a couple of weeks ago in a moment of fun but now it was the gold standard for every time Piers came up to the nursery.

"Again! Uncle Piers, please! One more time!" Emerson begged.

Piers complied and twirled the child around like a merry-go-round and again gently flung him onto the bed.

"Whew! You weigh a ton. Did you grow since yesterday?" Piers asked.

"Yes, Sir. Everyday Celine says I'm getting bigger," the small boy said with a huge smile.

"Well, good," Piers said in playful-seriousness. "Emerson, I talked with Mr. Chattersworth and he told me he met a young chap down by the fox trap named Tallant. Wouldn't know him would you?"

"Yes, I do. We played together yesterday. Celine says if I bring him to meet her, we can have a lovely tea with cake and crisps."

Piers shot Celine a knowing grin. "She does, does she? I think that's a grand idea, Emerson, but I want you to stay in the house today and until I say it is okay for you to play outdoors again. It's important for you to follow my directions. Do I have your word you will stay indoors? Celine may take you to town to play at the village park to make up for it."

"That would be wonderful, Uncle Piers! I love the play park. My friends from school go there on Thursdays. May we go tomorrow?"

"I leave that to Celine to decide."

Turning to her, he said, "I'll be out for a dinner tonight and I need to check afterwards on The Grange, so please keep Emerson indoors and have a pleasant evening. Set the alarm. Thank you."

"Have a nice evening, Mr. Cousins, and I'll do as you say," she replied.

"Good night, Emerson," Piers said. As he was leaving the room, a small tap on his hand made him turn around to see the boy standing close and gazing up at him with big, questioning eyes.

"What is it Emerson?" he asked.

No answer from the child, but he wrapped his arms around Piers' legs in a tight hug.

A sensation he'd never known before gripped the man's heart. From his vantage point, he was able to see only the top of a curly blond head and the profile of a chubby cheek.

He reached down and pulled the child into his arms and hugged him for a long time. Short arms encircled Piers' neck and Emerson whispered, "I love you, Uncle Piers."

Piers' eyes stung and he said in a husky voice he hardly recognized as his own, "I love you so much, Emmy. I'm so lucky to have you here with me."

The little boy lay his head back and smiled up into Piers' face. "Can we play tomorrow, too?"

"Of course. Better be ready to play a big game of hide and seek. This old house has some great hiding places."

"I'll be there, if you'll be there."

"I'll be there. I promise."

The child squirmed down and ran over to Celine and sat at the small table again.

"Goodnight, I'll see you both at breakfast in the morning," Piers said and left the room. He ran back out to the car and got in.

"Is everything alright?" Helen asked.

"Everything," Piers said, leaning over and giving her a friendly peck on the cheek, "is beautiful."

CHAPTER 21

"I'M NOT HAVING ANY LUCK getting Albright to pick up his phone. I've left four messages," Johns said laying his cell phone down again.

He and Detective Richards were in Nottingham and leaving the forensic lab. They'd waited to talk with Jinks, the head doctor at the forensic lab, but she was called out on an investigation. Cynthia, who was her assistant, gave them the entire report on Laura Rossar-mescro's wounds.

The blade that killed Laura was slightly curved and extremely long. It pierced her chest wall nicking her aorta. She had only five to six minutes from the time she was stabbed to the time she died. If and when they found the Rossar-mescro's family heirloom sword, forensics would be able to match it with the wound.

"Her killer was close to the boat. Laura wasn't moving fast. I'm afraid we missed something or someone in all the excitement. He, or she for that matter, may have walked right past us after they stabbed her," Johns said. "Our men didn't find any sword or knife when they dragged the canal."

"I still think it must be someone who either knew the family or one of the Rossar-mescros. If they fell out over the letter or if there's some jealousy between clans, we may find the knife that killed Laura Rossar-mescro with another Romani tribe," Richards said. "Try Albright again, but if he doesn't answer, let's go get something to eat. I'm starving. It's past three o'clock."

Johns continued to get the answering machine, so he drove to Nandos and they each bought their food in the take-away line. Remembering Michael, the Chief ordered the promised meal for his Sergeant. Once back in the car, they drove to the address where Thomas Albright lived. As the two men got out of the car, Detective Richard's mobile rang.

"Chief, can I have a moment? It's my supervisor," Richards said.

"Sure, wait in the car. I'll be right back."

Thomas Albright's house was situated in a rural area outside Nottingham. A well-maintained garden surrounded the front of the dwelling but there was no sign of life about the place other than a comfortably chubby orange tabby cat sunning itself on a stone bench off to one side of the door.

"Anyone home?" Johns asked the cat affectionately scratching its head after he pulled the door bell rope.

For his mannerly approach, Johns was rewarded by the cat rolling onto its back and offering a view of its ample, furry belly. With paws in the air and a tail twitching every so slightly, the tabby waited for a respectable scratching.

"Hmm? I bet if I take the bait, I'll probably be sorry."

"Nah, I think you're safe, Chief," Detective Richards said coming up behind him. "This old fellow is needing some attention."

Richards leaned down and rubbed the cat's head between its ears and gave it a friendly tummy rub. The cat purred and accepted the human's act of fealty with the true grace and dignity of a feline. Once satiated, it rolled back to its sitting position, wrapped its tail around its front paws, hunkered down and with a contented yawn, shut its eyes. It assumed a statuesque serenity like the sphinx of old Egypt.

"He's not going to give us any answers. Should we leave a note?" Richards asked.

"You take the side around the garage and I'll check over here." Johns pointed toward the pretty bay window to his left.

The two men met again in the front after they'd finished circling the house.

"Nothing," Johns said in a frustrated tone. "Where would he be? Maybe we should talk to a neighbor."

"Perhaps he's on vacation. Helen Ryes said he was retired. I'll do a background check on him. There may be a wife, kids or a few mates," Richards offered. "If you don't mind, Chief, I need to make a few more phone calls. My supervisor wants a full report."

"Good idea. You get on that and let's get back to Marsden-Lacey. I need to meet the Rossar-mescros and tuck them into the safe house for the night."

Johns sighed as he opened his car door and sat down in the driver's seat.

"What is it?" Richards asked.

"I've got my work cut out for me. There are currently thirteen family members of the Rossar-mescro clan and that's not counting the two-year-old baby girl. Every one of them loaded up into a house with only four bedrooms. We need to solve these two murders fast, Richards. Those Romani will get bored after about twelve hours in lockdown."

"Where's the house, Chief?"

"An old farm not far from the village. Lots of room outside but not much inside."

Detective Richards was again nibbling on his leftover peri-peri chicken. "You didn't eat much, Chief. Why?"

"I'm saving it for later. Since I've got to move all the Rossar-mescros tonight, I may not get supper. Supposed to be at a dinner party tonight, but probably won't make it." He put the bag in the back seat and continued, "If I do though, I'll see Helen Ryes this evening. She may have some information on Albright. Probably should bring her along anyway when we talk with him."

Johns was thoughtful for a moment. "Isn't there some sort of saying about 'rest' and the 'wicked?'" he asked as the car pulled onto the M62 highway heading west.

"No rest for the wicked. That's the saying, Chief," Richards said, finishing his last bite of chicken. "But surely you don't mean us. We're the good guys, remember?"

Johns didn't say anything. He focused only on the road in front of him all the way back to Marsden-Lacey.

CHAPTER 22

THE BLACK AGA STOVE WAS doing a fine job of warming Polly's cozy country kitchen. There was a slight dusting of cornmeal on the old harvest table, on Martha's nose, and on the honey-colored flagstone floor directly beneath her. Martha was busy mixing up the batter for hushpuppies while Polly chopped and diced a colorful mix of peppers, onions and celery. A wonderful smell from a frying pan sautéing the vegetables along with garlic, cayenne, oregano, paprika and of course butter, heaps of it, filled the room with an aroma so mouthwatering that Amos hovered and whined until sausage tidbits were finally tossed to the floor.

"What about a nip of wine in that pan?" Polly asked Martha as she added some more green peppers.

"Oh we'll add it, but in just a minute. We've got to get our priorities straight, first."

Martha took one of the bottles of Pinot Grigio they'd purchased earlier, opened it and filled two ample-sized wine glasses, one for her and one for Polly. Raising her glass to her hostess, they lightly clinked them together.

Martha toasted, smiling broadly at Polly. "Here's to the meal and here's to the wine. May the first be delicious and the second sublime."

"Here, here!" Polly raised her glass to Martha. "I've got one for you now: may friendship, like wine, improve as time advances."

This camaraderie building continued for some time between the two chefs and they were well into their second copious glass each and feeling the effects, when a knock came on the front door.

Remembering the earlier threat of invasion, Polly swung around and announced in a slow slur, "Better get my pistol. You follow up with the shotgun, Martha."

"I'm right behind you," Martha said, searching around for their weaponry.

Michael, who heard the knock, came into the kitchen from the family room. "No, you're not and the both of you stay put in here. I'll get the door."

"Stand back, young man. Where's my gun?" Polly demanded. "I've got a right to protect my property!"

Taken off guard for a minute by the scrappiness and possible tipsiness of his commanding officer's mother, Michael hesitated momentarily about how to handle the situation. Polly, who was only about five feet tall and weighed twenty or so pounds more than her current age of seventy-two, took advantage of his uncertainty and with a quick kick to the back of Michael's knee, sent him stumbling off-balance. Tossing a handful of flour into his eyes, she rolled him onto his side and with her foot shoved him under the long table. Martha happily watched the events unfold with a sappy smile on her face.

The constable's stunned immobility gave Polly time enough to spy the guns on the top shelf of the side board.

"Get those guns, Martha, and let's see who dares to knock at my door."

Martha grabbed the shotgun, and smiling a bit crookedly, tossed it two-handed to Polly, who, with surprising dexterity, caught it and tucked it under her arm. Like two tipsy banditos, they staggered to the front door leaning slightly to one side.

Once at the door, Martha tried to see over her compatriot's head to see out the peephole, but found it difficult because Polly's hair, much like her son's, liked to stick straight up in places. Puffing wine-imbued air over the top of her short friend's spiky-grey head in order to see, Martha got tickled and started to giggle.

"Who's out there?" Polly asked feeling an infectious twinge of hilarity taking hold of her from Martha's goofy giggling.

"It's us, Helen and Piers. Are you okay? You sound… hysterical," Helen said from the other side of the door.

More snorting and tittering came from the inside. Some clanking, rattling of the door chain and some thumping indicated Martha and Polly were either dropping things or just having difficulty maneuvering the hallway. On their part, Martha and Polly were happily laughing and exchanging comments like, "not by the hair of my chinny chin chin" until they finally lapsed into snickering and all out guffawing while slipping to the floor up against the door.

"What is going on in there?" Helen demanded.

Finally, after a few minutes, the lock moved efficiently and the door opened to reveal a flour-covered, irritated Sergeant Michael Endicott.

"Come in, please," he said with a nod toward the bench seat in the entryway's alcove. He pointed to the two smiling rowdies. "They may need to drink some strong coffee, if you get my drift?"

Helen hauled Martha to her feet. "Come on, you. Time for something warm to drink and a cookie or two."

Piers assisted Polly and soon both female gunslingers were nibbling on toast, cookies and drinking coffee. As Martha and Polly simmered down, Helen went over to the stove where a nice tendril of steam lightly emitted from the sizable, cast iron stew pot.

"So, how's the cooking going?" she asked, lifting the lid on the jambalaya. "Oh, this smells wonderful, Martha. Where did you find the Louisiana style andouille sausage?"

Sipping on a second cup of coffee, Martha said, "You wouldn't believe what Mr. Murdock has stuffed into that market of his. I told him what I needed and he obviously has a huge crush on Polly, because he scampered off to the back, rummaged around and returned to the front with that sausage all bundled up nicely. No cost of course."

Martha winked knowingly at Polly who rolled her eyes in response.

"That old devil had the temerity to wheedle himself into dinner tonight," Polly said while pulling red pottery plates from a cabinet. "What was I to do? He used the andouille as a means of entry into my company. Wily, he is, as the day is long."

No one dared to comment on the obvious affection Polly harbored for the party interloper because everyone knew if she didn't want him at dinner, she would have tossed the sausage back in his face at the grocery and left the premises in a state of offended annoyance. Instead, she'd cocked an eyebrow and gave him a smile that would melt butter. Mr. Murdock eagerly promised to bring his best bottle of Champagne to the festivities.

“I’d better get going and lay the table,” Polly said. “Girls, let’s put those Waterford wine glasses out. That’ll gussy the table up. Help me take them from the cupboard.”

So, with many hands to bring the party preparations and the dinner together, it was to be an evening to remember. All that was needed was for the guests to arrive, merrymaking to begin, and the wolves to stay away from the door.

CHAPTER 23

PERIGRINE AND ALISTAIR ALONG WITH Comstock, their schnauzer, were finishing their preparations for the night's entertainment. Presentation was everything. Not that Comstock was attending the dinner party, but he would be staying at a sitter that evening.

Alistair put a traditional camel plaid with white, black and red argyle sweater on the all-black ten pound schnauzer. Later, the sweater would be removed because the dandy dog would be hot from the rough-housing and fetching games with the sitter's children.

"Isn't he the man-about-town tonight?" Perigrine said as Comstock came rattling down the wooden stairs to what they called their sitting room.

"He does turn out well when he's been brushed."

"Did you put hair product on him?" Perigrine asked, noting Comstock's spiky-gelled head.

"Yes, and a dash of cologne. A dachshund will be in attendance at the sitter's tonight. Wants to be his best," Alistair said while adjusting the crate full of things they were bringing to Polly's.

"So, you're packed and so am I."

"You have our clothes, shoes and lights? All the equipment working?"

"I do. Comstock can stay the night at the sitter's?" Perigrine asked.

Alistair put the leash on the dog. "All settled. We're ready."

The three highly groomed gentlemen left through the back door of the garden shop and walked along the back alleyway toward the constabulary. There, standing in an awkward group, were about fifteen people of varying ages with the most unusual collection of bags, baskets and crates heaped full of household items and clothing.

"That's the Rossar-mescro clan," Perigrine said quietly under his breath to Alistair.

"Better see what our Romani guests are doing. This could be in our favor," Alistair returned.

They walked up to Stephan who they recognized as the man who first spoke with Johns after arriving in the village. Comstock broke the ice with a hello yap which enticed the children to scurry around him and acknowledge his excellent taste in outerwear.

"Good evening, Mr. Rossar-mescro. How are you?" Perigrine asked.

"Not so well. We're waiting for Chief Johns to return. He's putting us in a safe place until the killer of my daughter is found," Stephan said.

Both P. and Al were silent for a moment. Alistair said, "So sorry to hear of her death. Do you know where you are going to be staying?"

"No, no. We wait here, but our boats are locked and safe. It's critical my family is kept out of harm. My nephew is inside telling the police we're here."

"Mr. Rossar-mescro, I think you should all be inside. They wouldn't want you out here in the open," Perigrine said in a gentle manner.

The Romani man's face tightened in concern. "Yes, you're right."

Turning to his kin, he said in a loud voice, "Everyone, pick up your things and follow me."

It was a ragtag bunch of people, including Perigrine, Alistair and Comstock, who piled into the Marsden-Lacey Constabulary. Children, a baby, two dogs, a smattering of adults and at least three teenagers. With their personal belongings in tow, they made themselves comfortable in the seating the small reception area provided.

Donna came around to talk with them. Cool and collected as always, she immediately took things in hand.

"Hello, Mr. Rossar-mescro. I'm glad you brought your family inside. We'll be taking you by bus tonight to our safe house. It shouldn't be more than another twenty minutes till we leave, so about six o'clock. Chief Johns is on his way back from Nottingham and wants to accompany you and get your family settled. Make yourself as comfortable as possible."

While Donna was busy taking names and directing traffic, Perigrine perused and flipped through the accumulated paper mess on the reception desk trying to make neat the never ending tide of faxes, files and sticky notes. Donna noted his helpfulness with a smile then the boys floated unobtrusively out of the constabulary and continued on their walk to drop off Comstock. They were quiet for a small distance.

"Better call it an early night after dinner. We need to get on those boats as soon as possible," Perigrine said. "By the way, I had an opportunity to see an interesting fax lying on the floor back there."

"Really?"

"The murder weapon that killed Laura Rossar-mescro may have shown up in London at an antiques dealer. Interesting note attached in that it was sold by a woman, very thin, brunette."

Alistair scratched his temple in a gesture of consideration of the information.

"The odd thing is the woman signed her name Helen Ryes, but the statement from the dealer says she had nothing particularly that stood out about her other than her perfume. He thought it reminded him of a strong perfume he'd smelled before, something like cotton candy. Helen wears Chanel."

"Oh, damn, Perigrine. We'd better check it out. Call the antique dealer tonight."

"Will do, but if it's who we think it is, I want you to do the talking, okay?"

"Fine, it's done." Alistair was quiet for a moment. He adjusted his bow tie with one hand. "The Rossar-mescro's boats will be watched over by constables from now on. Let's stroll down to where they're tied up tonight. Best to know the layout."

In a short ten minutes, the boys found themselves staring at three quiet canal boats tethered to bollards not more than thirty feet from The Traveller's Inn. No lights other than those from the inn and one flickering street lamp illuminated the surroundings. Standing in the shadows allowing Comstock to serve as their excuse for being out meandering about the village in the dark, Alistair and Perigrine discreetly watched the three boats for signs of life.

After ten minutes with nothing moving but the occasional frog scuttling across the water along the banks, they turned to go, thinking the boats were truly abandoned.

"Good evening Comstock!" came a fairly loud voice from the other side of a low wall which served as a fence of sorts for The Traveller's Inn's outdoor pub area.

"Oh, and you two as well, Mr. Clark and Mr. Turner," Constable Cross said leaning over the wall with a thermos in his hand smiling congenially.

"Why good evening to you, Constable," returned Perigrine. "A slight chill tonight, don't you think? Have anything of consequence in your thermos?"

"Sir, I'm on duty." Cross held up the thermos saying, "Nothing more than strong black tea in here. Waiting on my relief to arrive, then I can go home to dinner. How's Comstock tonight?"

Constable Cross adored the small schnauzer and the feeling was mutual. Normally, Cross was his sitter, but when Perigrine called, Cross mentioned he would be busy this evening.

"Round the clock, huh? They're working you fellows too hard Constable," Alistair said.

"Nah. It's good to have a job. What's that they say about rest and the wicked?" Cross asked.

The two older men exchanged subdued glances.

"I think it goes something like 'no rest for the wicked,'" Perigrine said softly.

"Peace," Alistair interjected.

"Peace?" Perigrine echoed.

Alistair nodded. "The saying actually goes 'no peace for the wicked.' Profoundly different meaning wouldn't you say?"

All three men mused on the adage quietly and waving good night, Alistair and Perigrine walked on down the dark village street.

"Better make that call, P.," Alistair said. "If it's who we think it is that delivered the murder weapon to the antique dealer, she's involved with some truly ruthless people."

"Didn't you just say it was 'no peace for the wicked'?" Perigrine said snippily. "She's a big girl. She'll get what she deserves if she's mixed up in all this."

"Perhaps, but you don't want to see her hurt. You love her. It would kill you."

Perigrine's only response was a grunt pregnant with annoyance. They continued their walk to the sitter's house in moody silence. Only Comstock maintained his earlier bright enthusiasm for the evening ahead.

CHAPTER 24

AFTER DROPPING OFF RICHARDS AT his temporary lodgings, Johns managed to round up the Rossar-mescro clan onto the rented bus. It was no small feat to transport an entire family and their things, but after a quick word of caution to Stephan and another to the constable who would be staying with them, Johns was finally free to head home to his own farm where the dinner guests were already enjoying themselves with cocktails.

"You're home!" Polly called out when she saw her son emerge from the low lights of the entry hallway. Everyone turned and welcomed Johns with happy smiles and greetings.

"I'm so glad you made it, dear, and it's only seven-thirty," Polly said, coming up close to her son and dropping her voice to a conspiratorial whisper. "Do you see who's over there?" She pointed to an older man who was dapper right down to the small carnation in his button hole.

Johns regarded the octogenarian Polly was pointing out. Mr. Murdock, the grocer, sported a red bow tie and extremely bright white tennis shoes. Catching Polly's eye, he sent her a flirty wink.

"Mr. Murdock is here and I may need you around. He may try to get frisky with me."

Johns stiffened. "I think I need a drink, Mum. Smells like something is burning."

The tactic worked and Polly hastened back to the Aga to check on her meal. Johns saw Alistair tending bar and made his move in that direction secretly wishing his mother had a better filter regarding the things she felt comfortable sharing with him.

"Would you like a drink, Chief?" Alistair asked. "We're having something Hemingway is known for." Alistair was in every way the elegant maestro of the cocktail bar. Both he and Perigrine were in black dinner suits.

"Good evening, Mr. Turner. After my last conversation, I need one," Johns said and scanned the room for red hair. Nothing.

Feeling underdressed, he added, "I'm sorry, I didn't get the memo that this was a black-tie event."

Piers walked over holding a tall, slim glass with a milky-green opalescent liquid inside, smiled at the Chief and said, "The decision to dress was impromptu, Merriam, and doesn't carry weight when one, such as yourself, is dedicated to a higher purpose."

"Sorry, Cousins, but I would disagree entirely," Alistair said as he poured a jigger of absinthe into a Waterford stemmed glass. "The decision to dress, some would say, is what indicates one's dedication to a purpose."

Piers laughed and tipped his glass to Alistair's sagacity. They were joined by Helen, dressed in a deep purple colored dress with a scoop-neck reminiscent of Grace Kelly.

She held a delicate piece of stemware in her hand filled with a white wine. "How are you, Merriam? Did you get to visit with Thomas Albright today?"

"I haven't been able to run him to ground. He's not answering his phone or his door. Does he travel much or would you know of any close friends I might contact?" Johns asked.

The pretty brunette's face turned slightly dark. "Did you see…perhaps sneak a peek in the windows?"

Johns knew immediately what she was concerned about. "No bodies anywhere in his house, well, at least not that I saw." A feeling of frustration, or was it foreboding, began to creep upon him, but he didn't have time to dwell on the condition of Thomas Albright's health because Helen moved swiftly around him. A slight sensation akin to static electricity tingled through his being.

"Martha! You're gorgeous," Helen said.

Johns turned around. For a split-second, he lost control of his facial expressions. There, in a sleeveless black cocktail dress with a v-neck and an above-the-knee gathered chiffon skirt, was Martha, stunningly beautiful. She wore a wide black belt and her red hair was pulled up in a loose chignon with soft, curling amber tendrils falling loose to lightly touch her shoulders. A brilliant green jade necklace, coupled with her white skin and red hair, glowed in the soft light.

Forgetting the presence of others, Johns made three quick strides toward her. "You are beautiful." His voice sounded far away.

"Thank you." She smiled, gazing up at him.

With all his heart, he wished they didn't have to stay at the dinner party.

"Here's your drink, Chief," Alistair said at his side, bringing him grudgingly back to terra firma.

Johns stared down at the green colored bubbly drink. At its rim perched an extremely slender wedge of lime stabbed through with a sprig of thyme. “What’s this masterful concoction, Mr. Turner?”

“Death in the Afternoon. A mixture of absinthe and champagne. It goes well with creole food which is what we’re having tonight.”

“If you would please take your seats, dinner is ready,” Polly announced.

The dinner guests moved into the dining area and settled into their places.

Transformed for the evening, the farmhouse table resembled something seen in decorator magazines. White table linens and the red pottery plates coupled with light-catching Waterford crystal stemware. Polly was using her grandmother’s silver. Two multi-armed candelabras graced the table allowing the guests to enjoy the soft glow of candlelight.

Relaxed conversation and occasional laughter, both light and uproarious at times, mixed with the soft tinkling of silverware touching plates or crystal brushing crystal. Perigrine mesmerized the dinner guests with a story about an abandoned manor house in Prague he and Alistair found themselves staying in for a few days years ago.

“Did you think it was haunted?” Martha asked, her expression hopeful.

“Definitely,” he said smiling thoughtfully. “It was rumored to have treasure buried within its walls. You would think it hadn’t been touched in sixty years. Dust covered the floors, the window sills, and the old crystal chandeliers.”

Helen put her napkin down beside her plate, indicating she was finished. "Surely you weren't the first people to cross the threshold in all that time?"

"No, others were more than willing to hunt for the diamond cache the original owner, a wealthy entrepreneur, supposedly hid from the Nazis as they marched on Prague. The owner was collected and sent to a death camp. He never got back to his home."

"Who's the ghost?" Martha again tried to bring the story back to the hoped-for haunting.

"His daughter. According to locals, she was extremely beautiful and as the armed men pursued her through the mansion, some threatening what they would do to her, she ran to an open window on the second story and threw herself from it. They left her body where it fell and for many days the local people were too afraid to come near the house. Finally, one of her childhood friends, a young man, stole into the grounds and buried her in the garden."

"Have people seen her?" Helen, as enthralled as Martha, asked.

Perigrine shot a glance at Alistair who said, "You started this. I'm staying out of it. I refuse to acknowledge it was anything more than moonbeams hitting the mirrors."

Perigrine shrugged and finished his tale.

"It's not so much they see her as that they hear her, but Al and I did have a moment in the upper story gallery, which if you asked me to go there again late in the autumn with all the trees bare of leaves and the moonlight filtering through the dusty windows, I'd probably decline."

"Oh, come on, man! Tell us what you saw," Polly demanded.

The table of guests unconsciously leaned in closer to hear Perigrine's finale.

"We were sleeping on bedrolls in a room overlooking the garden where she is supposed to be buried and it was a foggy night so when I awoke from a sound, the first thing I saw was dense fog outside the windows. The moonlight created a luminescence intensifying the brightness in the room. Alistair was snoring about five feet away so I rolled over and pulled the bedroll over my head. I was now facing the hallway."

No one moved. Like children telling ghost stories around a campfire, they waited for the final reveal.

"That's when I saw her. She stood in the door, staring at me, wearing a dressing gown and nothing on her feet. Her face was so pitiful and sad. That's when I heard footsteps. She turned and with one last glance, she was gone. I pulled myself from the bedding and moved as quickly as possible to the door where I'd seen her standing. There was a faint, barely audible cry and it was taken away by the scratching of branches outside."

"Did you see if she was outside?" Piers asked.

Johns chuckled.

"What? I love a good ghost story, too," Piers said unapologetically.

"No, because the footsteps sounded so real, I was sure other people were in the house. My mind wouldn't wrap around the vision other than it had to be someone trying to scare us."

Perigrine lifted his wine glass and took a drink. "I turned to go back and wake Alistair, but—"

"I was already out of my bed roll," Alistair said. "It was time to go."

Alistair's tone was blasé.

"Ah, come on Alistair. Did you see anything?" Martha needled him.

Leaning back in his chair, the strangely handsome man's dark eyes gave nothing of his inner thoughts away. Instead, Alistair changed the subject, which was something he was extremely deft at doing.

"I only heard the wind and voices in the garden. Real people's voices. We needed to leave. Someone turned the polizei onto us. We never found the diamonds."

Johns shook his head, but he was smiling when he said, "Oh, what I wouldn't give to know a quarter of the things you two have been up to in your…line of work. Which brings up something interesting."

Perigrine and Alistair gave the Chief their full attention along with the others at the table.

"I think I may take you up on translating Rossarmescro's letter, Mr. Turner. We can't find Thomas Albright so we've sent a copy of the letter to Scotland Yard to have it translated and for forensic testing, but in the meantime I don't see a problem with having you do a quick read, if you're still interested?"

"Absolutely, Chief. Happy to help," Alistair said as he sat his wine glass firmly on the table.

Just then, Amos, who had been busy working the underside of the dining table for possible crumbs, growled in a low, menacing way.

Helen peeked under the table to see what the fuss was all about just as glass shattered inward from the kitchen window accompanied by an ear-piercing explosion.

Johns yelled, “Get down! Everyone down!”

Helen froze in her chair. Piers grabbed her and pulled her to the wall under the window. When Martha heard “down,” she scrambled under the table only to meet Perigrine and Alistair under there. A bullet ripped past Polly’s head, nicking her ear and causing her to fall to one side of her chair. Martha reached over and pulled her to the center where they all huddled on the floor littered with broken glass.

Johns called out, “Is anyone hurt?”

“Your mother’s been nicked but—” Martha answered, cut short by a blast ringing through from the living area.

Perigrine moved first, crawling from under the table and neatly turning out the dining room lights, leaving only the candles to illuminate the space.

Johns, in a hushed voice, said, “I want all of you to crawl toward the pantry. Who has their mobile phones?”

“I do,” Piers said.

“Call the emergency number and tell them it’s the Chief’s house.”

Piers reached up, grabbed some napkins, and offered them to the women so they could wrap their hands to protect them from the shards of glass.

They moved quickly to the pantry and once safely inside, it was Martha who asked, “Where’s Alistair and Perigrine?”

Johns yelled, "Turner? Clark?" No answer came. "Where the hell did they go?"

It took some time before sirens were heard coming toward the farm. Johns instructed everyone to stay put until the area was declared safe. As the constables surrounded the area and checked barn stalls, the back garden shed and the outlying fields, it became sickeningly apparent that whoever fired on the dinner guests was a professional, most likely a team.

It was only thanks to Amos' growl, which had caused Helen to bend down to look under the table that their intended target was still alive.

"Did you see where Turner and Clark went?" Johns asked Piers.

"No, too dark, and I wasn't paying attention. I'm sorry."

Johns said in a firm voice. "This is much bigger than what my constabulary is able to handle. We're dealing with professionals and whatever they're after and didn't get, they'll be back. I think I need to put the girls in police protection. I should have done it already."

The muscle in Piers' jaw flexed. "If anything happens to Helen, I'll see to it the men are tracked down and…"

"What?" Johns demanded.

Piers didn't answer. He left the room to presumably find Helen. Johns turned to see Martha's fearful face and her red hair hanging tumultuously from its chignon. He held out his arms and she allowed him to embrace her.

"It'll be okay. I promise," he said holding her tightly.

Across the field and toward the river Calder two slim figures hurried down to a boat. They were being watched by Alistair and Perigrine who, after the motor started and the small watercraft made its way toward Marsden-Lacey, got up and headed not back to Johns' house but to where their car was parked down by the entrance to the farm.

Looking at his watch, Alistair saw it was already ten o'clock. "We're running out of time."

"Let's get to the boats and pray they haven't figured it out yet," Perigrine responded.

They moved quietly and found their car. Within ten minutes they were on their way to The Traveller's and three slumbering narrowboats waiting for destiny to finally come knocking.

CHAPTER 25

STANDING IN THE DARKNESS OF his room, Emerson scanned Healy's front lawn with the telescope he and Piers were learning to use. With the rain over, the bright harvest moon could be easily seen. More white than yellow, it crested above the tree line brilliantly illuminating the wet grass causing the lawn to sparkle whenever moonlight touched the millions of tiny water droplets. A few wisps of fog were beginning to unfold their tentacles and wrap around the trunks of the massive oaks down near the river Calder.

He saw Mr. Chattersworth coming back from the far stretch of field where the fox trap was hidden. Earlier that day, Emerson heard the old gamekeeper mention that he would be checking that evening to see if the trap worked. The boy hoped the fox didn't take the bait. Tomorrow, if Celine was up to the walk, they would explore the area and if the fox was in the trap, he would set it free.

Emerson continued to watch the lawn. He controlled his breath to keep his vision steady. That's when he saw it. Another smaller figure came out from behind a massive oak trunk. It was Tallant, his new friend from the boats. Emerson knew Tallant was going to try and save the fox by setting it free.

The thrill of a night's adventure easily suppressed any objections Emerson's conscience tried to make regarding safety. He quickly put on his shoes and a jacket.

Grabbing his backpack, he shoved in a flashlight, his iPod and all the cookies he'd been saving from teas for the last week. They might need rations, if the night was long.

The only trick would be eluding the dogs outside, but if Chattersworth was mucking about they must be in their kennel. Without so much as a squeak from his bedroom door, Emerson let himself out. Down the long, shadowy corridor to the staircase, he went on tiptoes, trying with all his might to not make a single sound. Celine and the rest of the household would be sound asleep.

Like all children, Emerson knew his surroundings well. Household systems and the physical layout of his home he'd learned by simply paying attention to what the adults around him were doing daily. So, being a bright boy, he memorized the security code to turn off the alarm system by watching Celine or Piers operate it.

He typed in the four-digits and pressed off and waited to hear the click. Within minutes he was running across the long, sloping lawn of Healy toward the Calder, his new friend, and a trap made for foxes.

Scene Break

"I WON'T GO TO NOTTINGHAM," Polly said staunchly. "Put me in one of your holding cells at the constabulary. I'll be fine there."

"Mum, I've already texted Detective Richards to come get all three of you and take you to a safe house in Nottingham."

The entire dinner party of guests, minus Perigrine and Alistair, were gathered in the living room. Helen and Martha were standing close by one another with their shoulders touching. There was a certain comfort that comes from knowing your best friend is close.

"Would you accept the idea of Helen, Martha and Polly coming to Healy?" Piers asked. "I've an extremely advanced security system in place plus there are the dogs."

Helen and Martha exchanged quick glances. They well remembered the stealthy German Shepherds which patrolled the grounds of Healy.

Not responding at first, Johns said, "Cousins, if they go to Healy, I need your word they won't leave. They typically don't listen to…directions."

"Of course. You have my word," Piers said, nodding at Johns.

"Fine, that would be more comfortable for them, but tomorrow we'll need to make better arrangements for their safety. I'll send Richards another text and tell him to hold off and that they are going to Healy for tonight."

"Um, out of curiosity, what were you going to say a minute ago about what we don't typically listen to?" Martha asked with her eyes suspiciously narrowed.

Johns pressed his lips tightly and smiled more with his eyes. "Authority. I was going to say, you don't listen to authority."

"I think I may speak for both of us," Helen shot a look at Martha who appeared to be on slow boil, "when I say Martha and I are going to check into a nice hotel."

Martha nodded her consent.

"Absolutely not!" Johns and Piers stated in unison.

Taken off guard by their uniform response, it was Piers who pushed on first. "Helen, there is no need to take a hotel for the evening. You will be comfortable at Healy."

The girls exchanged glances and Martha said, "You're kind to offer, Piers, but we'll manage at a hotel fine. Thank you but we'd only be putting your household in danger."

"I'm going with them," Polly said matter-of-factly, "if you'll have me?"

The girls both laughed and Martha said, "Sounds like fun. Still have your gun, Polly?"

"Polly, you're welcome to come to my house. I'd be honored to protect you," Mr. Murdock said with a gentlemanly bow.

Polly pursed her lips together. Giving Mr. Murdock a critical eye. "I don't think so, Murdock. Good try. I may consider allowing you to escort me to the Neighborhood Watch meeting tomorrow, if you don't try any funny business."

"Delighted to be of service," the disheveled dandy said. "I'll pick you up in my car."

Johns grumbled. "You're the most stubborn women." He stalked off to other duties but not before calling over his shoulder, "I'm sending a constable to sleep outside your doors."

Martha flicked Helen a "whatever" expression and they followed Polly upstairs to pack their things.

"Helen," Piers said, causing her to turn around. "I would feel better if you would stay at Healy tonight."

She turned back to him. She saw his worry in his face and his affection. It humbled her momentarily. When Johns turned to Piers for his word, it was as if the two chattels had been neatly shifted from one man's responsibility to another's. She wouldn't be dealt with like that ever again.

"I appreciate your kindness and your generous hospitality, Piers. You are a dear man, and we're even. You saved me tonight." She gave him a pat on the arm and standing back. "I am going to stay in a hotel with Martha and Polly. The thought of bringing more danger to Healy doesn't set well with me. We'll be fine."

Piers' face showed a sliver of frustration. He gave Helen a quick, terse smile and said, "I'm going to run by The Grange to check on things. If you need me, I'll be in town for a short while."

Helen hoped she'd not appeared ungrateful. She was fine and she enjoyed being in control and wasn't going to relinquish that authority to anyone ever again.

He nodded. "I get it. Johns was right."

"About what?"

"Stubborn. He said you are both stubborn."

Helen laughed. "Damn right we are, but in all the right ways. I'll give you a call tomorrow. Thank you again."

"For what?" he said.

"Being such a good person, Piers."

He studied her face for a moment. "No one's ever said that to me, Helen."

She cocked her head toward her shoulder and said, "They missed the *best* part of you, then."

Helen, with a short wave, walked out of the room to go pack her things.

Piers watched her go and, in a hushed voice, said, "No, that part wasn't there before…you."

CHAPTER 26

"CHIEF? IT'S WATERS. I HAVE two pieces of good news for you. Dr. Billings, the forensic specialist at New Scotland Yard, faxed a file regarding the document we sent down. They've translated the letter written in Russian."

"Donna, send a copy to my phone but read me what the translation says," Johns said.

Donna read:

> *"I, Sotnik Ivan Ivovich Lysenko, of the Leib-Guard for Her Imperial Majesty The Empress Dowager Maria Feodorovna, left Russia on May 23, 1917.*
>
> *The Empress' items I retrieved from the barge that left Kiev are in safe keeping. I am not able to return to My Empress. She is under house arrest in Yalta. I have made it to England and wish to see the items safely in your hands. I am ill and probably dying. This letter I entrust to this woman, a friend, Sophia Argintari, to bring to you along with the following items:*
>
> *Empire*

Blue Hen
Cherub
Mauve

Your faithful servant,
Sotnik Ivan Ivovich Lysenko"

Johns' mind was in a whirl. No wonder people were trying to kill the Rossar-mescros. They must have something extremely valuable in their keeping that belonged at one time to The Empress Dowager of Russia. He didn't know his Russian history well, but he did know the Romanovs lost everything during the Bolshevik Revolution. Was this something belonging to them? Who was this letter meant for?

"What do they say about the carbon dating of the paper? Does it match with the date on the letter?" Johns asked.

"Yes, they put the carbon dating at between 1915 and 1920 for both documents. The document analysis done has DNA residue from two distinct individuals. Dr. Billings says it will take time to work with the Russian consulate to match the one sequence, but the other sequence matches Laura Rossar-mescro's DNA sample."

"What is the other good news?" Johns asked.

Donna, with suppressed excitement, answered, "I'm sorry I didn't get this to you earlier when you came by to relocate the Rossar-mescro's but Sam must have taken it off the fax machine and forgot to tell me."

"I'm going to pull that boy's up by the scruff of his neck the next time I see him. What did the fax say?"

The murder weapon that killed Laura Rossar-mescro may have turned up. It was offered to an antique dealer in London yesterday. He bought it and according to the officer I spoke with on the phone, if it is the actual weapon, it's a valuable piece. But here is the best part. It has an inscription: Leib-Guard, Sotnik Ivan Ivovich Lysenko."

"That nails it, Donna. It has to be the murder weapon. Any description of who sold it to the dealer?" Johns asked as he stood outside watching Endicott and Cross hammer an old piece of wood over his blown out kitchen window.

"Yes, a woman in her late thirties. Wearing sunglasses. Her brunette hair was pulled up in a bun. The man said he'd remember her perfume if he ever smelled it again."

"How was she paid?"

"Diamond necklace," Donna replied.

"What? A diamond necklace? Did she take it in trade?"

"Yes, but she did have to sign and you'll never guess the name on the signature line."

"No," Johns said shaking his head in frustration, "but make my day and tell me what the signature says."

"Helen Ryes. The signature says Helen Ryes."

For at least five seconds Johns didn't say anything. He stood staring at the unattractive wood paneling they found in the barn to cover his mother's kitchen window. He said, "Did they get prints on the weapon?"

"Yes, they did, but they need to run them through Interpol," Donna replied.

"I'm bringing in Helen for questioning and fingerprinting. Don't share this information with anyone else at the station. I'll be there in twenty minutes."

Johns ended the call and flagged Sergeant Endicott over.

"Helen Ryes left yet?" he asked.

"No, Sir. She's in the kitchen with your mother and Mrs. Littleword."

"Good. I think it's time to find out more about our Mrs. Ryes."

Johns headed to the front door of his house. With each step he took, he mentally connected another dot. One person was at the center of every conversation and every event: Helen.

As he emerged from the dark entrance hall into the light, he saw the three women standing around the table. They turned toward him.

"No hotel tonight, ladies. I'm taking you to the constabulary. You'll be safe there."

"We said we would get a hotel." Helen's tone indicated a slight annoyance.

"Not an offer," he said pausing for effect. "Let's say it's more of a…necessity."

His tone indicated it wouldn't serve to argue. Opening the door and standing to the side so they might pass in front of him, Johns waited. One by one Helen, Martha and Polly walked outside into the dark. It was going to be a long night.

CHAPTER 27

THE AUTUMN EVENINGS IN YORKSHIRE can turn cool, especially close to the water. A low mist was forming above the river Calder creating eerie twisting shapes whenever the soft night wind blew down from the higher hills. Seemingly indifferent to the breeze's frigid bite, Perigrine and Alistair, unrecognizable in black clothing and face masks, sat hunkered down within fifteen feet of the Rossar-mescro's three boats still moored below The Traveller's Inn. With each breath of wind, soft tinkling sounds came from the small bells tied into the lines, keeping evil spirits from settling on the Romani's water homes.

P and Al had sequestered themselves behind a long row of hedges bordering the canal. They kept a vigilant outlook for any unusual movements along the old tow path. Perigrine, wearing a pair of night vision binoculars strapped to a type of head gear allowing him to keep his hands free for the evening's work, barely breathed as he scanned the dark environs up and down the canal.

"Nothing and no one is about, Alistair. Should we go?" he asked in a soft whisper. "It's getting late, almost ten-thirty,"

"One minute," Alistair replied. "Here comes Constable Cross moving toward the boats for one last inspection. He should be expecting a relief officer soon.

Once they're talking, I'll release the lines to the black boat and you be ready to board the blue one."

The goggle-head nodded. The sound of a car door slamming beside the inn made their heads jerk slightly to see who it was. Constable Cross called out a hello and soon they saw another police officer walking up to the outdoor dining area. He was chafing his hands together trying to adjust to the cold. The two constables talked for a while and moved to the back door of the old pub as if they might go inside.

"Go!" Alistair hissed.

Perigrine moved cautiously, staying within the shadows of the foliage along the river's embankment. Al ran to the boat farthest away from the potential view of anyone left inside the inn and lay flat on the ground. At this angle it wouldn't be possible for anyone standing up on the pub's patio area to see the embankment's edge below.

In a hunkered run, Alistair untied the boat's rear lines and tossed them onto the back deck. He moved to the bow end and untied the other set of lines, slinging them onto the front deck where they landed with a quiet thud. The boat, free from its restraints and shrouded by the mist, did the bidding of the river's current and quietly slipped away from the embankment and floated downstream without a sound.

By the time both constables disappeared inside the pub, Perigrine was already on board the blue narrowboat and using the night-vision goggles to work the lock on the door to the living quarters. The latch turned over easily letting Perigrine slip safely inside the cabin unseen.

Alistair scrambled back to the red boat landing lightly like a cat on its deck. Putting on his own pair of night-vision head gear, he moved with feline agility to the boat's aft end and picked the cabin's lock. Again, it gave way in less than a minute and Alistair gently stepped down into the cabin and shut the door behind him. He touched a slim metallic gadget clipped to his chest. This two-way radio paired with Bluetooth headsets, allowed the two men to communicate with one another.

"Are you able to hear me?" Alistair asked.

"Perfectly," responded Perigrine. "You?"

"Perfectly," Al answered. "Keep to the sweeping strategy we planned. The boats are from the same builder so their layout must be similar. We probably should expect some hoopla once the third boat is discovered gone. Should give us time to search these two from top to bottom."

With a delicate hand and a consummate attention to detail, they gleaned each boat for its potential hidden secrets. Success depended on sticking to their plan of meticulous investigation. Lifting cushions, searching inside mechanical holds, tapping interior walls and discussing the renovations done by the family, gave them a precise map of the entire boat. Because the Rossar-mescros had lived on these boats for over seventy years, upgrades would be normal consequences of changing times and technology.

For the most part, the boats retained their original charm, but there was nothing indicating poverty or want in the Rossar-mescro's lifestyle. The appliances were all relatively new and the interior was well-maintained, and other than the old tiffany-styled dining lights probably original to the boats that still hung over the cozy sitting banquets, the rest of the electronics, lighting and furnishings were homey, up-to-date and in excellent condition.

Perigrine heard it first. His movements ceased all together and he whispered into his microphone, "Someone's outside. They aren't on the boat…yet."

No response from Alistair. Perigrine waited as still as a speck of dust in a library.

"Don't move, P. We've got company and it's not the police," Alistair finally answered.

A sound came from the deck of Perigrine's boat. He spoke hurriedly into the tiny microphone, "I'm heading to the rear of the boat to the main bedroom. There's a door there. I'll take care of this one."

"Remember, we can only bag the trash," Alistair said.

"Of course."

Perigrine waited. He'd found a perfect hiding place on top of long shelving which ran the length of the aft bedroom cabin above the wardrobe. Easily hoisting himself upward, he settled his long, skinny black frame in a side-ways position resembling a tidy bed roll waiting to be retrieved from its snug shelf. Digging into a small zippered pocket, he pulled out a handkerchief and a thimble-sized plastic bottle filled with a clear liquid. All was quiet.

Soon, he heard the subtle sounds indicating another life was in the boat. He waited making himself calm and ready, being careful to not exude any energy which the other person might sense. As the boat's floorboards creaked with the weight of an approaching body, Perigrine unscrewed the bottle and waited to soak the hanky with the liquid inside.

A tall figure moved into the room and hesitated momentarily. Approaching the drawers, it rifled through them and once done, it lifted a few pictures hanging on the walls. The silhouetted form switched its attention to where Perigrine lay and opened the wardrobe, digging around directly beneath him. As the person shut the doors and turned around facing the bed, Perigrine leaned over, grabbing the person's throat in a choke hold, and lifted him off the floor while pressing the handkerchief to his face. The body struggled and slapped at the air wildly, but went limp in less than twenty seconds. Perigrine let the person slip quietly to the floor.

"One down," he whispered into the microphone.

Not getting an answer from Alistair, he knew to wait and listen intently for any indications that another person was on board. Nothing. He lifted the man lying on the floor up under his arms, and dragged him to the bunk. Once there, he rolled him in the blankets to secure him from moving even if he did wake up.

In his ear, he finally heard, "I'm outside, P. My pig's in its blanket. Meet me down behind the mill. We need to see where our other boat floated to." Alistair sounded out of breath.

"There in a tic," Perigrine answered lightly.

Within three minutes, he stood in a cold misty night near the five hundred year old Marsden-Lacey mill. Nothing stirred the serenity of the scene. The village was as quiet as one might expect it to be on an autumn night with everyone sleeping deeply in their beds.

A movement beside him and a wicked chuckle let him know his best friend was enjoying his nocturnal adventures, too.

"What did you do with yours?" Alistair asked.

"Put him to bed. Should be sleeping comfortably when the police arrive. By the way, we should make a phone call."

"Already done. Did it while I was on the boat. Let's take a hike before the police arrive. The new constable who came on duty will be Johns' favorite chew toy for a few weeks. He's nowhere to be seen. We'd better get moving. It's already eleven-fifteen."

"Why didn't we find anything? Do you think they moved them into a bank safety deposit box?" P. asked as they walked along the path, careful to hug the shadows.

"I've inquired around and the Rossar-mescros do have a bank account, but it's in London. My gut tells me they don't even know what they have. The boats hold the answer."

The boys took off downriver. Their steady strides halted for only a minute to turn around to see a commotion of lights and men yelling behind them. Car floodlights and sirens whipped the calm, nighttime environment into a whirlwind of activity. Voices called to one another and officers poured over the edges of the two boats.

They saw Johns stomping around on the embankment pointing downriver, but P. and Al were safe from detection in the foggy gloom of the tow path's thick, overhanging vegetation.

The lost boat would be hunted and, once found, hauled back to The Traveller's Inn and inspected. Perigrine and Alistair hoped it would continue to float unencumbered until it was caught in the back-current of the first bend of the river right near the embankments of Healy House.

The boys needed to move fast and even though Perigrine and Alistair were motivated by mercenary intentions, they still always tried to give back to their community. It was going to be Christmas-come-early for the police force of Marsden-Lacey. Al and P. had thoughtfully left two pretty presents handily wrapped and tied for the constables to find once they inspected the Romani's boats. Presentation was everything, Alistair would have said, if he'd been present at the discovery. Currently though, he was busy. He and Perigrine were on their way to a rendezvous of sorts with the last boat in the Rossar-mescro fleet: the Empire, and punctuality, in their game, meant the difference between life and death.

CHAPTER 28

BEING OUT AT NIGHT WAS a revelation to the child. All his senses were working double-time and the feeling of freedom was exciting. The darkness didn't scare him. Instead he was more aware and alive. It was cold but his youth and his expensive outerwear kept any real threats of exposure at bay. The flashlight's beam flicked around as he made his way closer to the fox trap. He knew Tallant would go there as soon as Chattersworth left.

He heard the sound of whining and a cry like a baby or a woman coming from the wood to his right letting let him know the fox was probably in the trap. He turned off the path, moving the hanging fir tree limbs aside to pass deeper into the undergrowth.

The light from the torch was weakening so he turned it off to save the battery in case he needed it later. The moonlight was more than enough for him to make his way.

Emerson heard the sound of metal on metal like a latch being scraped against something made of steel. He hesitated, feeling the hair on the back of his neck lift. Instinct told him to stay still. Without breathing, he hunkered down in the spot where he stood being careful not to make a sound with his feet or his body brushing up against surrounding vegetation.

He waited. Footsteps circled the fox pen and occasionally the poor wretch caught inside would chirp and whimper. Emerson knew when it was best to stay quiet and small. It didn't pay to draw attention to himself when his late father had been in earshot.

"Shut up you mangy beast!" an unseen man hissed. The sound of something hitting the wire fencing and bouncing hard against the ground made Emerson flinch. It wasn't old Chattersworth's voice. The child crouched down into a small ball, completely invisible under the low swags of the massive fir tree's limbs.

From his left, a white pebble rolled quietly between his feet and emerged right below his gaze. Turning his head slowly to see Tallant, also tucked down, Emerson began to speak. The older boy gestured with a finger over his lips for Emerson to stay quiet.

"The women didn't show up," a man's voice said.

"One of us should wait. We need to get rid of her. She's the only one left who can recognize you," another man said in a strange accent.

"I can't spare you. We're wasting time. Those boats will be inspected tomorrow or worse, they'll be moved. Let's get back to the village and help Victor and Pete."

Three sets of legs walked past the hiding children and along the edge of the wood. As soon as Tallant and Emerson saw the figures disappear above the slope line, Emerson spoke. "Who was that?"

Tallant whispered, "I don't know, but one is a cop."

"Should we release the fox?" Emerson asked, returning to the reason he'd come out in the first place.

A grin broke out over the Romani boy's face, revealing perfectly white straight teeth and a healthy set of dimples framing the corners of his smile. "Let's do it."

Scrambling out from under the fir tree's protective limbs, Tallant and Emerson quietly walked in the direction of the fox trap. As they approached the enclosure, the fox gurgled and made the guttural noises known to its species.

"Hush there, little one. You'll be free in a moment," Tallant said, talking in a low, even tone. The animal picked up on the boy's quiet, gentle energy and soon settled down near one of the far corners of the trap.

The wind was picking up, moving the fog out of the river valley. As the dark-haired boy lifted the latch on the trap's gate, the night sky cleared and the moon's bright light shown down, bringing clarity to the landscape. The two boys, distracted for a brief moment by the sudden brilliance of nighttime's beauty, gazed toward the river where moonbeams made the water's surface sparkle with white flakes that undulated with the ever-moving current. Like a mythological creature summoned from the mist by a dark wizard, a black elongated shape like a great beast emerged from a shadowed bend in the river.

"What's that?" Emerson whispered with a twinge of awe.

Tallant didn't answer. They both studied the silhouette's movement, waiting for its true identity to reveal itself. It was Tallant who realized the truth first.

"It's a boat. It may be one of ours."

"Let's go see," Emerson said, excited by the thrill of investigating this new mystery.

"First, let's set the fox free."

Tallant pulled the gate open and the boys stepped away so when the animal was ready, it had a straight shot to scamper out of the hateful trap. They watched as the fox hesitated and carefully tucked itself deeper into the corner of the enclosure. It seemed uncertain of whether to trust the two human enough to pass in front of them.

The two boys didn't wait. The fox would leave once they were gone. With light hearts and aided by the strong light beaming down from the bright moon, they ran the short distance to the river's edge and studied the boat caught in the strong back current.

"It's the Empire and she's somehow floated all this way," Tallant said. "Come on, Emmy. Let's get on the boat. I know how to start the engine. With your help, I can take her back up the river."

Emerson thought for a moment. "Won't those men be looking for it there?"

"Yeah, that's right."

The two boys were quiet for a while trying to think through their problem.

"What if we tie the boat up next to the embankment under those willow trees? It would be hard to see it in the darkness with the limbs coming down over it," Emerson said.

"I like that idea. Come on let's get to work."

Waiting for the boat's bow to rub up against the embankment, Tallant leaped and grabbed the guard rail. He clung to the side with both hands and with the kind of agility best exhibited by strong, fearless young boys, olympic gymnasts and highly-trained navy seals, Tallant flipped himself onto the deck of the Empire with ease.

He tossed one of the boat's lines to Emerson who, by using one of the willow tree trunks as a simple pulley, was able to slowly pull the boat to the shore. Once the bow bumped against the embankment, Tallant jumped onto the ground and tied the boat securely by its lines to two willow trees hugging the edge of the river.

"Would you like to come on board, Emmy? I know where my Mum keeps the biscuit tin. I'm hungry. Are you?"

"Yeah, starved. I've brought us treats, too."

Inside, Tallant pulled down the stained glass lantern hanging over the dining banquet and, striking a match, lit the lamp's wick. The soft glow from the light made the boat's interior cozy and warm. With attention to detail, Emerson and Tallant went around to each porthole window and pulled the heavy curtains closed, thereby effectively sealing the lamplight within the cabin.

Emerson saw the oven clock's time. "After I have a biscuit, Tallant, I'd better get back. It's already eleven-thirty. Celine might wake up and miss me. She'll take away my DS for a week if she finds out I slipped out of the house."

"Okay. I'd better walk you back, Emmy. Those men might be hanging about."

Emerson sat in the corner of the banquet nibbling thoughtfully on his biscuit. "I don't want to run into those men. Do you think we might be able to start the engine and drive the boat down the river? There's a dock below Healy. I can see it from my window. If we make it there, I might be able to get back into the house and pretend to be asleep."

"It's worth a try," the ever-capable Tallant said. "Finish up that biscuit and help me release the lines. I've been driving this boat since I was six, so not to worry."

With the confidence of old deck hands, the two young boys neatly untied the lines and got the boat's engine started. They maneuvered the craft from its hiding place. Tallant knew how to handle the steering wheel like a true pro of nine years and soon under the moon's benevolent light, the Empire and her crew bravely headed downstream to the port of Healy.

CHAPTER 29

"DOES ANYONE HAVE A HOT water bottle?" Polly asked while standing in her robe and house slippers. She was making herself comfortable in one of the constabulary's cells for the night and was busy preparing her accommodations for a comfortable night's rest. She'd given up going to a hotel simply because the only hotel she would want to stay at was run by her friend, Tessa, and if she woke Tessa up at this time of night, Polly would never hear the end of it.

Donna was the only real constable left at the station as every other officer had rushed off to the river to search for the missing boat. Sam kept her company most evenings, and he was still with her even though it was now past eleven. It was already past the end of her shift time and Sergeant Cross would be there soon, allowing Donna to head home.

Readying herself to leave, Donna simply shrugged at Polly's questions and pointed her to the officer's lounge where she might find almost anything in one of the many over-stuffed, gadget-filled drawers. With a resigned air of a capable woman who had spent years multi-tasking the jobs of children, family, work and housekeeping, all needing something at once, Donna went back to her present thankless job of soothing Helen's ruffled feathers.

"I'm leaving, Constable Waters. Chief Johns has no reason to hold me. I've told him everything regarding my whereabouts yesterday. Martha has vouched for me," Helen said, indicating Martha sitting on one of the tattered reception room chairs.

Martha was painting her nails a flaming red color. The tableau of frazzled red hair, discarded shoes and Martha lounging back on a mangled feather pillow sporting Garfield's cartoon face, didn't exactly engender reliability and confidence in Helen's argument regarding Martha's credibility. Exchanging expressions of uncertainty and awkwardness, the two women returned to their debate.

"Mrs. Ryes, trust me, I would let you go, but I'm waiting on the Chief's answer. He left so quickly that he didn't get to finish getting your statement. I don't have the okay to release you. It won't be long, but I do need you to please be patient." Packing her purse, Donna was ready to leave for the evening.

"Are you going home?" Helen asked in an incredulous tone. "Who's going to run this place once you're gone?"

As cool as ever and completely unruffled by the night's high intensity and Helen's circumstances, Donna picked up her favorite coffee mug, smiled comfortingly and said, "Sam's here until midnight but not to worry, Sergeant Cross will be here soon. I'm locking the constabulary so you'll be safe."

Putting her plaid coat on and slinging her purse over her shoulder, Donna continued, "Do yourself a favor, Helen. Pour a nice cup of chamomile tea, lay down on your cot and relax. You won't do yourself any favors going on like this. The Chief will get back with us as soon as he can."

Briskly making her way to the front doors of the constabulary, Donna flashed Martha and Helen an upbeat smile, waved goodbye and disappeared out into the dark. In less than a minute, Helen watched Donna's car weave through the narrow entrance to the constabulary and melt away into the fog. Sam walked over and locked the door. Giving Helen a shy smile, he meandered back to his desk and sat down to fiddle with his phone.

She knew when she was beat. With a great sigh, Helen turned to see Martha still performing her make-shift manicure. The room reeked of nail polish.

"We're never getting out of here, Martha. This is absolutely ridiculous. Why am I all of a sudden a suspect?"

"Helen, my dear," Martha said with a deep sigh, putting another dab of red lacquer on her index finger, "You're not a suspect. Merriam is just pushing his weight around. I'm working on it. Cool your jets and go check on Polly. I want to make sure she isn't nipping on that brandy we know Johns has stashed in his office. It's time pistol-Polly is in bed."

Throwing her hands up in the air, Helen went in search of the Chief's mother.

Martha held out her hand to appreciate the final color on her nails and deciding it met her satisfaction, she smiled and perused the room to see what else was going on. Sam Berry was the only person left and he was busy texting on his phone.

Martha's affection for Sam was great. It hadn't always been so, but Martha and Helen owed Sam a debt of gratitude for saving them from an icy death and this rectified any earlier problems between them.

"How do you like working here, Sam?" she asked, getting up to come over where he was sitting. Finding a comfortable chair across from him, she sat down.

The tall, handsome young man blushed lightly and replied, "I like it, Mrs. Littleword."

"Sam," she rebuked him gently while blowing on her nails to dry them, "you know you're to call me Martha. We're beyond the formalities. Saving someone's life has a tendency to toss all that to the wind."

Her gaze lifted from the hardening shellac and she considered the pressed uniform and the clean shaven face of the once shabby Sam. "I heard you're working on your course work for the junior officer program. That's fantastic."

With a big smile at the warmth and encouragement in her voice, he said, "I am and I will be going to Manchester for more training in March."

Martha beamed. She enjoyed young people. "You're going places, Sam. How will your Aunt Harriet not to mention your girl friend Penny, get along without you?"

The glum face returned, but this time his manner indicated he wanted to shake something off. "Uh, I'm actually not seeing Penny anymore, Mrs…I mean, Martha. There's someone I'd like to get to know better, but she is way out of my league."

Martha cocked her head to one side and regarded Sam. "I don't think anyone is out of your league. You're a good person. What makes you like this new girl so much, Sam?"

He hesitated for a moment then said softly with awe in his voice, "She's beautiful."

"Inside or outside?" Martha asked in her matter-of-fact way and waited for the reply.

"Outside for sure, but I don't know much about the inside. I haven't been able to talk to her much."

"What you *know* isn't enough," Martha said simply. "A woman of any substance won't tolerate being liked, or loved for that matter, for her beauty alone. What's her name?"

He didn't offer the name immediately. Martha waited.

After some hesitation, he said the name. "Celine. Her name is Celine Rupert. She's Mr. Cousins' new nanny."

Martha shook her head. "Dear, dear Sam. I've met the charming Celine, and she isn't someone who'll appreciate anything less than true sincerity. You're going to have to look deep inside yourself and ask a few hard questions. Like what you find special about her. She's beautiful, that's true, but she won't be interested in someone who only sees that side of her."

Sam nodded, and with a sheepish grin said, "Thanks, Martha. I'm learning to listen to the advice of older women."

"Ooh, you're going places. Smart man, Sam."

Martha patted him on the shoulder and got up to go collect her things over by the couch. The desk phone rang startling them both making them laugh at their own jumpiness.

Sam lunged for the receiver saying, "I'll get it."

"Hello, Marsden-Lacey Constabulary. This is Sam Berry speaking."

A flush of red bled up into his cheeks. "Yes, we'll send someone right over."

Sam hung up the phone and jumped up from his desk. He radiated intention. “That was Celine Rupert at Healy House. She says Piers Cousins’ young charge has gone missing. They need help finding him. Supposedly Detective Richards is already there, but they need help.”

Sam’s moment was nigh. Martha saw the surge of hope fill him with the valiant spirit of a chivalrous knight. His lady love needed him.

“Slow your horse down there, Galahad. You can’t run off and leave your post tonight. Do you have anyone else on duty?” Martha asked.

For a moment, uncertainty flashed across Sam’s face, but all was good again in less than a second. “I’ll leave you with the key and you lock the door. Everything will be fine. One of the night constables will be here shortly. They know Donna’s schedule.”

Like an excited puppy barely able to restrain itself for the sign it was okay to dash out and play, Sam watched Martha for her consent to go, whether it be verbal or facial.

An idea fostered by opportunity and encouraged by need dawned on Martha so she said, “Sam, give me the keys and I’ll lock up. You go to Healy and help find Emerson. Get going.”

With a massive smile of joy on his young face, the boy levitated over the banister and pitched the keys behind him as he bid her adieu. He was gone in less than five seconds. Martha, as the temporary warden in charge, tossed the keys a few times into the air and, with a sassy swing of her hips, walked over to the main front doors of the Marsden-Lacey police office and neatly turned the main lock, effectively securing those inside, inside, and those outside, outside.

"Helen!" she called, turning and making her way down the hall to the holding cells. "Let's roll! We've been sprung!" With a mischievous smile playing on her lips, she added under her breath, "I said I'd lock up the constabulary, and I will, but I'll be on the outside when I do it."

CHAPTER 30

"CROSS!" JOHNS BELLOWED, MAKING ALL the other constables flinch as they continued their work to stabilize and protect the crime scene near The Traveller's Inn. The night was getting long and the police officers were weary from lack of sleep.

"Sir, Cross left," a young constable named Evans answered.

"Left? Why in the ever-loving-world would Cross leave?"

"Um, it was his turn to man the constabulary, Sir," came the tentative reply.

"Oh. Where is…"

But before the Chief barked another order, a cry came up from the lower dock area where the remaining two boats were still tied up.

"Chief, we need you down here. We've found two men gagged and tied on the boats. They're alive," yelled one of the officers from the deck of the two narrowboats left tethered to their bollards.

"This night just keeps on giving," Johns muttered as he descended to the lower ground. The investigation team was doing an excellent job. His phone rang. It was a number from Nottingham Police Station.

"Chief Johns, this is Dr. Townsend in Nottingham. Do you have a moment?" a female voice said on the other end of the phone, forcing him to stop his stride downwards. He grimaced.

"Yes," he said in an irritated way.

"I wanted to share some evidence with you regarding the Laura Rossar-mescro death. It's late but we thought it might be handy information to have going forward on your investigation."

His interest piqued, Johns stuffed his colicky attitude. He would make a concerted effort to be pleasant. Holding up his index finger, he turned back to the young detective and yelled, "Detective, restrain the two men you've found and bring them up to the detention van when it arrives."

Dr. Townsend continued. "I know you spoke with Cynthia when you came to Nottingham and she gave you a complete update on our findings thus far. However," she paused, "we didn't have data back on the fingerprints from the sword used to kill Laura."

Johns waited and prayed it wouldn't be Helen Ryes' prints.

"Did they get a match?" he asked.

"Yes, two actually. There was one thumb print matching a Ukrainian hit man named Victor Holub who goes by 'The Dove.' Cute, huh?"

Johns nodded and braced himself for bad news. "And the other set?"

"That was the interesting set. They belong to someone who has a restricted access which means it's probably not going any further until we hear back from the Secret Intelligence Service," Dr. Townsend said.

"Thanks, Doctor. I appreciate the information."

Johns thanked her again and headed to his car and logged on to the Police National Computer, a database of criminals and their descriptions. He wanted to read about Victor "The Dove" Holub.

There was plenty of information on the Ukrainian hired gun and his earlier career working for Polish Military Information Services. Holub had dropped out of sight after the reorganization of Poland's Secret Service in 2006. Out of a job probably due to a shift in alliances, he must have gone rogue and worked for the Russian mob. The database's picture was probably ten years old, but it would do. Johns got out of the car and assessed the investigation scene, noting the arrival of the armored police van.

"Are they in there?" he called to the two uniformed officers standing guard in the temporary police paddock roped-off by yellow tape.

"Yes, Sir," the taller officer answered.

Johns made his way along the outside of the roped-off paddock and over to the designated van. He knocked on the door. Michael opened it and moved aside for him to come into the small mobile unit. There sat two unwholesome characters neatly restrained at wrists and ankles. Neither showed interest in the comings and goings of the police officers. Instead, they sat in their chairs with expressions of boredom and annoyance.

"So, want to explain what you were doing on the boats tonight?" Johns asked while reading the papers Michael handed him. Not getting any answer, he locked eyes with one of the men. "Victor, I asked you a question?"

There was a tremor of movement in the mouth area of the strongly built, dark-haired man's face.

"So, nobody here is Victor 'The Dove' Holub."

Johns turned to Michael. "Sergeant Endicott, call SIS and get their people down here. I think once we run this one's prints, it's probably going to match the ones found on the murder weapon that killed Laura Rossar-mescro."

The dark-haired man exploded in his chair, writhing like a wild beast and toppling onto his side. He ranted in a foreign accent while twisting and kicking at the officers who tried to manage him. The other prisoner screamed at him using the same language, but it didn't slow his machinations to free himself. Michael and another officer did their best to subdue him, but it took five minutes of working with straps and tape to immobilize him completely.

Once Victor was back in a sitting position but disheveled and breathing hard, the other detainee said something to him in an eastern language resembling Polish. The tone indicated a threat and Victor grumbled, "Rozumiem."

Johns realized he wouldn't get any sort of compliance from the two men. They were professionals and whoever they were working for would rather see them dead than let them offer information to the police. So, Johns stepped back out of the van and told Michael to take two constables with him and put both of the detainees in holding cells at the constabulary. He would get the SIS to send their people. Victor was a real prize for them and they would love to get their hands on him.

Outside, he lifted his gaze to the night sky. There in the clearing of a cloudless, star-filled heaven, he threw up a grateful thank you to the person or persons responsible for delivering to him the two mongrels responsible for killing Laura and possibly Sharon O'Connor as well.

The wind picked up and blew the mist down the river valley. Johns huddled deeper into his macintosh coat and strode to the boats floating like two brightly colored toys brilliantly lit by the enormous utility lights the police set up to see their work area better.

A young constable named Evans walked up to him and said, "Sir, the inside of the boats are in good condition. Things are disheveled, but there's no damage. They were looking for something."

Johns stepped across the gangplank and down into the cabin of the blue boat named the Blue Hen. The room was messy but undamaged. He continued to the back of the boat, making a note of the bed covers strewn around the cabin.

He wondered if there were competing parties involved. The boats needed to be impounded. Whoever had rifled through them, must be searching for something very valuable. The big man sighed and ran his hand through his bristly hair in a gesture of uncertainty. His cell phone rang. It was the constabulary. "Yeah. This is Johns."

"Sir, this is Cross. I'm at the constabulary and a couple of things are going on I thought you might want to know about."

Johns rolled his eyes heavenward and chewed his lip.

"Well, don't keep me waiting Cross. I can barely stand the anticipation."

"Sir, Stephan Rossar-mescro is here and one of their children, Tallant, is gone. The two women you had requested to stay the evening, Mrs. Littleword and Mrs. Ryes, are not in the constabulary anywhere and…"

Johns' blood pressure began to simmer. "What?" he asked incredulously. Why was Martha Littleword the most difficult woman he'd ever met? Why did she continue to push his blood pressure to the boiling point every time he dealt with her? With no answers coming from either the divine or from his own wearied brain, Johns sighed and said in a subdued tone, "Finish your story of woe, Cross."

"Um, well, Sir. Sam is gone and it appears there's another missing child at Healy, Emerson Carstons. The note on the night sergeant's desk is written in a florid style and it smells of gardenia."

"Martha," John said in a low growl through almost gritted teeth.

"What, Sir?" asked Sergeant Cross.

"I said, that Littleword woman bolted and she's God knows where. You'll need to be ready for some detainees. Endicott and Evans will be bringing them in. I'll go to Healy and find out what is going on. Put Mr. Rossar-mescro in an office. I've got two men being brought in and I don't want Stephan to see them yet. It's possible he'll be able to identify one of them. Tell him to wait there at the constabulary. There's a good chance the two boys are together."

Johns thought a short minute before he continued. "Cross?"

"Yes, Sir?"

"The two prisoners being brought in are extremely dangerous. I don't want anyone to know they're being detained. No one except you, Endicott and Evans. Tell them to keep it quiet. If the Secret Intelligence Service shows up tonight, they're the only ones other than you three who may have anything to do with the prisoners. With special precaution, get Rossar-mescro to see if he recognizes either man. Got it?"

"Got it, Sir."

"Good. Oh, by the way, I'm pretty sure Sam's at Healy. He's been trying to find a reason to charge over there all week. If he shows back up, send him home immediately."

Chief Johns hit end on his phone. He dialed Martha's number and counted the number of rings trying with each one to get control over his blood pressure. He heard the phone click.

"Don't be mad, Merriam," she said. "We aren't on the lam. Helen and I heard about Emerson. We could do more good helping at Healy than sitting in that ridiculous cell all night. Your mother is asleep in cell number one, by the way. Tucked in like a bug in a rug. She found your brandy, so she probably won't be in a good mood in the morning."

Why was it whenever he heard her voice, his resolution dissolved into mush? Johns tried to work up his irritation again to at least sound firm. "Martha, you and Helen left without being released from custody. What is wrong with you? There's a murderer on the loose."

"Merriam, there wasn't anyone at the constabulary. I felt like a sitting duck and Helen's worried about Emerson. Hang on a minute," Martha said in a rushed, tense tone. "We've pulled into Healy and three men I don't recognize are signaling they want to talk with us. Hold on a minute."

"Martha?" Johns hurriedly said into the phone, but all he heard was a garbled conversation.

She came back on the phone. "Merriam, I think there is something strange going on. Those men were acting extremely weird. I didn't stop. One is a constable you've been working with a lot. I need to call you back. Helen is trying to tell me something."

"Martha, do not hang up the phone…"

The line went dead and he stared dumbfoundedly at the phone. He dialed again but only a busy signal blared annoyingly through the phone's speaker. Frustrated by the random twists of technology, he told himself to be patient. The universe rewarded his choice to not over push and the phone rang.

"It's me," Martha said. "I needed to hear what Helen was trying to tell me and I wanted to put some distance between me and those men. Something about the way they were acting and how they tried to bend down to see in the car."

There was a brief moment when Johns heard Helen's voice. She sounded unsure. Martha came back on the phone.

"Helen says one man is a dead ringer for Thomas Albright, you know, the man she told you about?"

Johns' stomach dropped and at the same time he realized the situation was a colossally horrible one. He needed backup at Healy, he needed to keep the boats safe, two children were missing and now he needed Martha and Helen to be safe.

"You two are in danger, Martha. Which man are you talking about?"

"It was the older detective you had with you this afternoon."

Was it true? If Martha and Helen were right, Richards was Albright. Albright must be after the Romani, too. How did he get past security at Nottingham? Johns' brain went into overdrive. He wouldn't take a chance letting the girls go back the way they'd come.

"No," Johns said, "but you are to go on to Healy. I'll be there in twenty minutes."

"We'll see you there."

The Chief walked firmly to the police utility vehicle. He flipped on the blue emergency lights and siren. The police vehicle jerked forward and picked up speed. Somewhere in the dark grounds of Healy a group of dangerous men would stop at nothing.

Johns had seen his fair share of those in positions of authority abuse their power for nothing more than money. On the other hand, he thought to himself, if Richards or Albright was a cop that had gone bad, there would be no mercy for him from his fellow officers. That, in Johns' book, was the vilest form of betrayal: a dirty cop.

CHAPTER 31

PIERS' CAR MOVED EFFORTLESSLY ALONG the tight curves of the road. His mind worked out the details of his last two conversations with Helen. He'd been involved with so many women in his life. Most of them incredibly beautiful and dying to have his attention. Helen was more than all of them rolled up into one. She was an exquisite gem but cold like one in some ways, too. He wasn't sure if Helen was pretending to be indifferent to spike his interest, or if she was set on the notion of only wanting his friendship.

He wasn't interested in friendship. The more she resisted him, the more he wanted her. This evening made it undeniably clear how much she meant to him. He shifted down into third gear, increasing the power of the car to climb the hill faster.

Not since Emilia had anyone made him feel this way. The thought of Helen made his blood burn in his veins and her constantly pushing him away was driving him crazy. The car topped the hill and shot down the other side giving Piers a small rush and some satisfaction at least in the unconditional speed and handling his car offered him.

A tinkling sound over the car's sound system indicated an incoming call. He saw the time of eleven-thirty, blinking on the dashboard's screen. Touching the answer button on his steering wheel, he said, "This is Piers."

Celine's voice was hysterical. "Mr. Cousins, I've been trying to reach you."

"I must have dropped my phone in the car when I went into The Grange. What's wrong?"

"Emerson slipped out of the house. He turned off the security alarm. I can't find him anywhere. Oh, my God! I'm so sorry!"

The girl was crying and as she finished, he heard another voice in the background.

"Celine, calm down. He's probably gone to check on the fox trap. Where is Mr. Chattersworth?"

He heard her talking to someone, a man, about if he'd seen the gamekeeper, Chattersworth.

"Celine, who's there with you?" Piers asked.

"It's a constable who was sent here to watch over some guests you've invited for the night," she answered. "It's Detective Richards. He's going to help find Emerson."

Piers put his foot down with a firm pressure on the accelerator making the car jump forward into a new realm of speed. "Celine, I'm just now leaving the village. I'll be home in ten minutes. Stay in the house."

The hedgerows and the silhouettes of trees flashed past as his car flowed through the claustrophobic tunnel of vegetation flanking the road. Like a thunderbolt exploding above him, Piers' instinct slapped him in the face and he knew the fear all parents feel at least one time in their lives: his child was in danger. The truth came to him with each word reverberating in his brain like a heartbeat. If there were predators in the woods, Piers realized, it would be the human kind.

He dialed his phone and counted the rings. One, two, three… "Hello," came Chattersworth's sleepy voice. "That you, Mr. Cousins?"

"Chattersworth, get up. Emerson is missing. Bring Kaiser to help. This is just the situation for a well-trained German Shepherd. Wait for me in the front drive with two rifles and two horses."

"I'm half-way there," Chattersworth said and hung up.

CHAPTER 32

CELINE, FEELING MISERABLE, SAT IN the high-backed chair next to the inglenook fireplace in Healy's main hall. She wasn't able to drink the tea Senior Agosto placed for her on the dainty tea table to her left.

"All will be fine, my dear. The child will be found and no worse for wear, as they say," the gentle man was saying in an effort to soothe her. "I, too, was a boy and I tell you it is normal to slip away and have adventures in the night. Emerson will be back soon."

Celine had come to love Senior Agosto even though he was high-tempered and difficult at times. But where Emerson was involved, she knew he enjoyed creating beautiful masterpieces for the child's teas. Tempting sandwiches in shapes of bees, flowers, and even boats were forever gracing the delicate child-friendly china plates sent up from the kitchen. Sugar-a-plenty and the best cream for the tea were never skimped on by Healy's master of confectionary eloquence.

"I know, Senior. I feel like a fool and if something should happen to Emerson, I would rather die than see him lost or…"

There was no finishing that sentence. The poor girl broke into sobs and Senior Agosto, completely flustered by someone else's high emotional state, sat down and gently patted Celine's hand, with a beseeching glance heavenward for assistance.

The front door swung open and banged against the brass floor stop, causing them both to jump. It was Sam Berry, a bedraggled knight errant come to slay whatever dragons Celine might deem necessary. She stood up.

"Can I…I…help you?" she asked.

Sam strode across the room, taking Celine off her guard by his handsome, earnest face. "I took the call about the child being lost. My superior officer sent me to help. Do you have any idea where he may have gone?" Sam asked, barely able to look Celine directly in her beautiful but worried eyes.

Uncertainty clouded her face. "We think he's gone to the fox trap. Mr. Cousins should be here any moment. I'm confused because the constabulary already sent an officer, but he left."

Sam's eyebrows furrowed but he didn't let the news of another officer weaken his own position. "I'm happy to help any way I can. Do you know if the child took any personal items with him?"

"No, but I think he took his backpack." The sound of a vehicle's tires on the gravel outside switched her thoughts and attention to who was arriving.

In less than a minute, Piers walked in with a take charge attitude. His jaw was set in a firm hardness.

"Where's Chattersworth?" he asked.

"In the kennel area waiting for you," Celine replied. Her voice raspy with restrained emotion.

"Is the constable with him?" Piers asked.

Celine and Agosto glanced sideways, redirecting Piers' focus onto Sam.

"Sam has come to help. The other constable left."

"That's odd," Piers said, "but Sam, thank you for coming. I'm sure we can use your help."

To both Agosto and Celine, he said, "There will be no special cakes, sweets or privileges for one week starting tomorrow for Emerson. He willingly disobeyed. Do you both understand?"

They both nodded. Celine more earnestly than Agosto, who first pursed his lips indicating he didn't absolutely agree, but finally assented only after Piers stared him down.

Celine began to cry softly. Sam's moment had come. He quickly picked up her phone that had fallen to the floor and handed it to her. Gently taking her by the elbow, he said soothingly, "Come sit down Miss Rupert. We'll find him."

He guided her to the tall wing-back and waited for her to sit.

Huge tears continued to pool in her pretty blue eyes and she again nodded. For a brief moment those eyes locked on Sam's.

"I'll bring him back. I promise," the boy constable said sounding more like a man with every word.

Piers was already moving toward the front door. "Come on, Sam. Celine, drink your tea. I'll be back soon with the little escapee."

When he swung open the door, there in the feeble light given off by two massive gas door lamps, Celine saw two dark bay Irish Hunters saddled and ready to ride with Chattersworth holding their bridles.

"Do you ride, Sam?" she heard Piers ask.

"I do."

The door closed on the scene. Soon the sound of hooves was heard heading away from the house. Celine thought about Sam.

Senior Agosto got up from his seat and bent down to pick up the tea tray. Celine put her hand on his arm to stay him from his purpose.

"Please wait," she said softly. "Let's have that tea."

She searched the kind face of the diminutive, older gentleman and waited. He nodded, sat back down and with quiet brevity, poured the tea.

CHAPTER 33

"THE BOAT IS NOT IN THE back current."

Alistair's statement sounded flat almost like he didn't believe his own eyes.

"It must have floated further than we expected. Well, one thing's for sure, it not far and it won't make it under the small bridge past the grounds of Healy," Perigrine said in a calm tone.

The two men had worked their way along the tow path and climbed the stile over the rock wall into Healy's estate. It was a short trip of only fifteen minutes from the place they'd left the police and the tied-up miscreants.

If Alistair's calculations were right, a narrowboat should have been ensconced in a lovely bend in the Calder near Healy where willows sweep the gentle current with their long, low branches. Unfortunately, not all plans are without their complications and this one had gone awry.

"We need to go on, but proceeding on foot will take all night," Alistair said. He'd sat down on the top of the stile and composed himself in a posture resembling Rodin's sculpture, *The Thinker.*

Perigrine leaned his tall frame against the rock wall and let one leg cross the other in a stance suggesting he was at total ease. In whole, they both appeared to be relaxed, thoughtful and nonplused by their perplexing situation.

"I've always wanted to drive one of those jet skis. This would be the perfect moment to jump on one and zip down the river to find the boat. We should have planned it better, Al," Perigrine reflected quietly while he pulled a piece of beef jerky out of his pocket and chewed on it.

Alistair leaned over, rested both elbows on his knees and scratched his right ear. "Bloody hell! I'm losing my edge, P. Ten years ago, I would have had a backup plan. I was so sure of that back current and the time frame. That's what comfortable living will do to you. Makes you soft."

Perigrine continued to chomp and chew unhurriedly on his jerky. "I once saw some chaps in Florida having a great time doing all sorts of tricks on jet skis. Someday we should go on vacation and give them a try."

Alistair turned to his old compatriot. "What's the deal with the jet ski fantasy? We're in a fix. I'm turning into a soft-minded simpleton and you're babbling about our next vacation."

He was quiet for a minute then added unhappily, "At least we have landscaping to fall back on."

"Oh, come on, Al," Perigrine said, fishing around in his pocket for more jerky, "it's always darkest before the dawn."

With a steady gaze at the nighttime sky, Alistair said, "Apropos, to be sure but…"

However, he went mute because there dangling from Perigrine's fingers were two sets of keys instead of more beef jerky.

"Shall we, *old man*?" Perigrine asked.

Even in the moonlight Alistair could see the excited glint in his friend's eye. "Absolutely!" Alistair jumped off of his perch on the rock wall. "I'm incredibly impressed, Perigrine. You saved our—"

But Alistair's last word would go unuttered. The cry of a nearby fox arrested their attention.

"It always sounds like a woman's scream. We'd better go. I'll follow you," he said.

"That'll be a first," Perigrine muttered mischievously under his breath as he tossed himself easily back over the rock wall's stile.

"You usually have to be the leader. So trying at times. Always having to think of everything."

"I can hear you, you know? Quit being smug." Alistair said without an overabundance of humor.

Perigrine motioned for Alistair to follow. Directly beneath where the wall met the river was a derelict boat house in need of repair. Anyone cruising along the river or walking the tow path, wouldn't pay much notice of it. Fortunately, Perigrine was a detail man, one who envisioned himself flying unrestrained across the surface of the river perched on the back of a powerful, agile jet ski.

It's a good thing dreamers dare to dream and smart people, if they're truly smart, keep their dreamy friends close by. In Perigrine's and Alistair's case, this piece of wisdom proved not only useful, but timely. Within five minutes, they were both sporting extremely jaunty grins and zipping up the river, feeling the wind stripping them of their weariness and concerns. As they rounded one of the curves in the languid river, they saw the object of their desire: the Empire coyly pulled up to the embankment near a small dock. She was well-tied to the cleats.

The boys, once they'd seen the boat, slowed their approach and their engines until they came to a full stop in the middle of the river. Alistair pointed to an area still in darkness along the river's edge not far from the dock. Slowly, they drove their crafts to the indicated spot.

For a time, they studied the narrowboat. Since someone had moved it there, it would be prudent to wait and watch before closing in on the boat.

"There!" Perigrine pointed to the dock. Scrambling out of the boat and onto the dock, were two young boys. They laughed and chatted to each other.

"How are you going to get home from here, Tallant?" the smaller of the two asked.

"I'm not far Emmy. The house we're staying in is over that hill. Ten minutes tops."

"I'd better run for it. I'll see you soon!"

The smaller child ran down the dock and jumped to the ground, leaving the other boy to watch him go. For a few seconds, it wasn't certain if Tallant would begin his own journey. He turned around and walked back to where the boat was tied up. With a surety to his demeanor, even obvious in the half-light of the night, Tallant checked the lines while he sang the same tune they'd heard the day the Romani arrived below The Traveller's Inn.

By the light of the empire,
By the light of the blue hen,
By the light of the cherub,
To the grave and beyond,
To the grave and beyond.

Finally, he turned to run down the dock and up the hill to the road. Within ten minutes, he would be back at the house, safe with his family.

Both Perigrine and Alistair watched him go. With engines barely humming, they approached the tethered boat. Staying away from the dock, they neatly hid the jet skis against the embankment and covered them with brush then headed on land to the narrowboat.

"What's that moving on the deck?" Alistair asked in a hushed voice coming to a dead stop.

"It's a woman but she's so unclear. She looking right at us and saying something."

"What's she saying?"

There on the deck of the Empire was a woman. Her words came floating across the water in a moaning sing-song way. "Mavia. Mavia," she repeated and then she was gone.

"Where'd she go?" Alistair asked.

"Into thin air, Al. Was it a ghost?"

"Absolutely not. It was probably the moon."

"When did the moon start singing words like Mavia? What does Mavia mean?" Perigrine chided.

"Maybe the Romani boy's voice carried and he said 'Mavia'."

"Perhaps."

They'd no sooner boarded the Empire, when they heard a scream.

"Was that a fox again?" Perigrine whispered to Alistair. "It sounded close."

"Wait. If we hear it again, I'll be able to tell."

A second more muted cry came.

"That's not good," Alistair said grimly. "Damn! We're going to have to check it out. It came from the direction where the small boy walked off to. Probably the kid."

The two men longingly gazed at the object of their night's quest so ripe for the taking, but instead hurried off into the darkness. Empire and all her promises of power and valuable secrets would have to wait. The innocent needed a defender. Fortunately for Emerson, he would get two.

CHAPTER 34

"MARTHA, I KNOW THAT WAS Thomas Albright. Something is terribly wrong. Why in the world would he be here?" Helen was saying as the Green Bean moved down the hill and into the valley where Healy sat like a dream under the bright moon.

"What if he's an undercover police officer or a spy?" Martha asked, working herself up with a vision of ruthless secret agents.

"Oh, come on, Martha. Those men he was with looked like criminals. Do you think he saw my face?"

Martha was maneuvering the Mini Cooper through the iron gates to the estate. "No, I don't but I do think he knew someone was in the car. He saw your legs so I'm pretty sure he also knows it was a woman."

Helen thought for a moment. "If that is Thomas Albright, why wouldn't he have owned up to it especially if he were a police officer working for Nottingham? Johns has been hunting for him for two days."

"If he's working for British Intelligence, he can't tell anyone, even Johns," Martha said and mused for a few seconds. "Would your friend Sharon have known him in a professional capacity?"

"Albright? Most likely she did. Our fields would overlap and everyone knew how to find translators for different things."

"I wonder if Sharon contacted Albright about the letter?" Martha asked, thinking out loud. She slowed the car to a crawl while they both mulled over the possible connections.

"If she did contact Albright about the letter, he may already know what it says."

"Why send the Romani to contact you, Helen? And why would Albright be standing in the way of the entrance back there?"

"I'm trying to remember what Stephan said to me the first time I met him. He said something about the woman from Nottingham 'pressing' the letter back on Laura. That sounds like she wanted to be rid of it. She may have been afraid."

Martha brought the car to a standstill and turned to Helen. With a penetrating stare, she said, "Ever get the feeling the dead try to communicate with the living?"

Helen, unnerved by the question, replied, "Like how?"

"Remember the story Perigrine Clark told at the dinner party about the young girl whose ghost awakened him that night in the old mansion?"

Helen nodded.

"I get the feeling, Helen, this situation is similar. If Perigrine hadn't been awakened by her, he and Alistair would have been caught. She saved them from the same plight she died from. From the minute you met Stephan Rossar-mescro you said you had an odd feeling about the man like you were being haunted. Remember?"

"I do remember the feeling of holding the letter. Like history was trying to tell me something."

"Maybe it wasn't history, maybe it was a ghost. It could have been Sharon or maybe someone who knew the Rossar-mescros."

"Whoever killed Sharon thinks I have the letter. They must want it terribly."

"Bad enough to kill Laura Rossar-mescro and most likely why we were shot at during Polly's party. They don't want anyone to figure out the letter. They think you already know and that's why they're trying to stop you. That letter must be very valuable in some way."

All of a sudden, Martha pressed the accelerator down, jolting the Mini Cooper into forward momentum and building speed like a Formula 1 competitor at the Monaco Grand Prix.

Helen gripped the door handle and pushed her feet against the floorboards to steady herself. "Why are you driving like a crazy woman?" she asked over the engine's growl while turning to stare at Martha to discern whether or not her friend had gone instantly insane.

The yew trees lining the drive whipped past and the shadows they cast over the speeding car blinked in rapid succession on the Mini Cooper's passengers. The bright moonlight and the darkness toggled back and forth, escalating Helen's anxiety.

"Because there's a car honing in on us," Martha said. "I can see its lights and they're moving even faster than we are. It can't be Johns because he left the inn only a few minutes ago, so it must be the men we were talking to. Something tells me, they put two and two together and realized you recognized them."

Helen turned around to see out the back window of the car. Coming down the first slope into Healy's valley were the headlights of a car flying at top speed.

"Martha, can't you drive any faster?" Helen asked, agitated.

Martha didn't take her eyes off the road, but her lip curled up on one side in a roguish smile and she pressed down harder on the accelerator. The Green Bean plunged forward, the velocity pushing them deeper into their seats.

"I've got an idea, Helen. Up at the last bend there's a curve to the right, remember?" Martha asked.

"Yeah, I remember. I think. Why?"

"If we go on to Healy House, they'll follow us. We can't have that. If I turn off my headlamps and swing the car into that nook, they might go on by. We can go back the way we came and hopefully meet Merriam along the road. What do you say?"

"Go for it."

Martha flipped the car's headlamps off. The moon's light was enough to see the road. As the Mini Cooper approached the curve, Martha whipped the car head-first into the snug, overgrown nook. With a cloud of dust hanging in the air outside, Helen and Martha both exhaled big sighs. They waited.

Light flickered on the shrubbery and loomed brighter until they heard the sound of an engine approaching. It didn't slow as it reached their hiding place, but instead the vehicle took the curve at breakneck speed, whipping the roadside vegetation around marvelously.

"They took the bait. We've got to move." Martha turned the engine back on without the headlamps. She eased the car out of its secret enclosure and revving the engine, took off back the way they'd come.

"Do you think we lost them?" Helen asked while keeping a sharp eye on her side mirror for headlights in the distance.

"For a short time. Call Merriam and tell him what we've done. Let's think of a place to meet him."

Helen dialed her cell phone. "Chief, we think we're being chased. We hope we gave them the slip. Can we meet you somewhere? The people who are after us went on to Healy so that's a no go."

"Meet me at the crossroad where the Calder runs under the bridge. Do you know the place?" he asked.

"Yes, we should be there in less than five minutes. Do you have a gun?" Helen asked.

"What?" he asked so loud that Helen jerked the phone away from her ear.

"A gun. Do you have a gun?" Helen repeated louder each time she said the word gun.

"You Americans! No. I don't and you two better not have one either."

Johns, on his end, was quiet for a moment. "Helen? Does Martha have a gun? Please tell me neither of you has a gun?"

Helen held the phone away from her mouth and asked Martha, "Do we have a firearm of any kind in the car?"

Martha shrugged. "I don't think so."

"That was vague. Do we or don't we have a gun in this car? Johns wants to know."

With one hand off the steering wheel, Martha did a quick finger-slash across her throat, indicating to stop the third degree. She said sweetly with her eyes blinking and in a stilted tone, “No, Helen. We do not have a firearm of any kind in our car. Why would we? We are two innocent women being chased by maniacs who want to kill us. Oh my! How will we ever protect ourselves?”

Helen’s eyes narrowed and her mouth tightened into a severely compressed lip formation. She replied to Johns who was still waiting for the answer. “No, Chief. We don’t have any firearms according to Martha.”

Martha rolled her eyes and silently mouthed the words, “goody two-shoes.”

“That answer took way too long,” Johns said. “Tell Martha she better turn the gun over on her own at the crossroads or I’m arresting her on the spot.”

Helen answered nervously, “Okay, I’ll tell her, but we don’t have a gun.”

“Give me that phone,” Martha demanded and reached for it. “Got to go, Chief. See you in five.”

Helen took the phone back, ended the call, and tucked the phone into the glove compartment.

“The gun in the back is Polly’s,” Martha fumed. “I didn’t put it in here, but I’m glad we’ve got it. He can have the old thing. It’s his mother’s anyway.”

“Where is it?” Helen asked.

“In the trunk in my bag. Hey, there in the river, you can see a narrowboat coming down in the dark.”

Martha pointed toward the river and a long narrowboat gliding on top of the black water. She slowed the car and pulled it over to the side of the road.

"They don't travel at night. It's not safe. Do you think it's one of the Rossar-mescro's boats?" Helen asked.

"It's docking."

The boat came to a stop and two small figures moved on the deck.

"Those are children, Helen!"

"What are they doing? That's got to be Emerson, don't you think?"

"We've got to get to the Chief. We need to tell him. Call Piers," Martha said.

Helen dialed Piers' number. He answered. "Piers, we think we see Emerson. He's on a narrowboat with another child. It's hard to know for sure if it's them but even from this distance, the smaller child's hair looks blonde."

"What a relief! I've got horses saddled. Where did you see them?"

"We're right above the Calder on the bridge that crosses it a few minutes outside of the gates of Healy."

"It's the old Healy dock. We're on our way. Thank you, Helen."

Helen ended her call and turned to Martha. "He's on his way now to get Emerson. Thank God, he's okay."

Martha picked up speed and in a few minutes they arrived at their destination to find Chief Johns waiting for them. He walked over to the car as Martha rolled her window down.

He said, "Girls, I'd like to read you both the riot act —"

"Hold your horses, Chief," Martha interrupted in a feisty tone, holding up her hand to quiet him. "We may have cleared one or two things up for you. There's a narrowboat floating on the river by the old Healy dock and two small children were on board. Might be Emerson."

She took a pause to breathe and when Johns thought he might get a word in edgewise, she held up a finger to stop him then continued her monologue.

"Also, the man you know as Richards is, in Helen's opinion, Thomas Albright. In my opinion, he may be a secret agent or vicious criminal. I'm probably right but I'll let you check it out using your police connections. And lastly, the woman who was killed, Sharon O'Connor, may have known Albright professionally."

Johns stood right next to Martha's window. He stared over the top of the low Mini Cooper's roof.

Martha reached up and grabbed him by his tie and pulled him down closer so his head was even with hers in the window. She planted a kiss right on his nose which, by the expression on his face, stunned him even more.

"That's better," she said with a twinkle in her eye and a big grin. "Did you have something to say?"

At least three different conflicting expressions crossed the Chief's face like clouds on a windy day scuttling across the sky. It was the last one that won the day though. With Martha still smiling up at him from her open window and her hand tight on his tie, Johns finally shook his head and grinned like a boy of twelve.

"You're something, Littleword," he said.

"That's what I thought you were going to say," Martha replied and pulled him in towards her again but this time she left off with the Eskimo delivery. No one complained.

CHAPTER 35

"GET DOWN," PERIGRINE HISSED TO Alistair who was coming up behind him. Having easily covered the ground from the dock to where they thought the scream originated, the two men studied the scene.

There, in a grove of ancient yew trees, sat Emerson with his two arms wrapped around his bent legs. Two beefy-sized men stood off to one side. One was on the phone talking.

"We found a boy. What do you want us to do with him?" one of the hulks asked in a rough eastern accent. He held the phone away from his ear as someone on the other end screamed something.

"Okay, I don't like it, but it's done."

The man put the phone in his pocket, saying something in Russian to his partner who kicked at the dirt with force.

"It's Cousins' child," Alistair whispered. "It doesn't bode well for the kid. I've got an idea. I'll double back around to the left side and draw their attention. Emerson isn't bound, so get him to run to you. Once you get him, run back to the boat. I'll catch up with you. Get ready."

Alistair slipped quietly off and Perigrine waited for what he knew would be coming. It was times like this that Perigrine remembered why he and Al enjoyed such a long association. Fun. They always had a lot of fun together.

"Who Who," called a particularly pathetic owl, sounding more like a bored ventriloquist doing a half-hearted job.

"What's that?" one tough asked the other.

Louder and with less enthusiasm than the first try came the repeat effort, "Who! Who! You morons!"

Both men took the bait and sprang out of the yew enclosure, giving Perigrine the chance to wave like a smiling, friendly savior to Emerson.

"Come on, Emerson," he whispered to the boy as loudly as he dared.

Emerson, not a dumb child by any means, furtively glanced at the brutes, and jumped up and ran to Perigrine.

"I know Mr. Cousins and I'll see to it you get back to him, okay?" P. assured the child.

"Okay," the boy replied simply.

Picking up the youngster and tossing him around to grab onto Peregrine's back like a monkey, P. ran for the dock.

Somewhere in the night a few thumps and a number of pain-induced cries emanated from a clump of ewe trees not far from the river Calder. The sounds were also easily heard by the ears of the powerfully built German Shepherd, Kaiser.

He growled low and stood in a posture of readiness. The finely-tuned ears pointed and twitched. His massive head turned toward the sound in the wood. Kaiser barked only once.

"What is it, Kaiser?" Piers asked eagerly, watching the dog's body movements.

Again, the regal animal barked and his stance spoke volumes.

"Seek!" Piers commanded from his seat upon the horse.

Excellent hearing allowed the powerful dog to quickly hone in on his prey's location. Like a lethal, noiseless bullet, he leapt forward into the night.

Scene Break

ON THEIR WAY BACK TO Healy to help join the search for Emerson and Tallant, the girls followed the Chief's vehicle through the main gates. They stopped right inside the grounds to get into Johns' utility vehicle. Scanning the landscape for the dock, the girls pointed in the direction where they hoped Emerson might be.

"The dock shouldn't be difficult to find," Johns said as he maneuvered the four-wheel drive over bumpy, difficult terrain sloping into the river valley. Fir tree limbs brushed against the sides of the vehicle. The occasional whack from a tree branch jarred their tired brains back into alertness.

Finally, the car emerged from the wooded terrain and they found themselves in a grassy pasture with a grove of ewe trees to one side and a few perfectly formed oak trees standing watch over the ancient meadow.

"Look!" Martha pointed to the stretch of river below. There with a soft beam of exquisite moon light pouring over its silhouette was the narrowboat. It sat peacefully beside the dock. No one moved upon its decks.

"Do you think the children went home?" Helen asked.

"Perhaps but there's one way to find out," Johns replied. "Let's go see."

He shifted down into a lower gear and slowly descended until, seeing a dirt road coming from the right, he was able to put the vehicle on a solid footing.

"This must be the path leading to the dock. If my calculations are right, we've doubled back close to the boundary line of the estate."

He pointed to a feasible spot to park the vehicle directly below on the slope. The river was wide in its bed along this section of the landscape. Gentle, open countryside spread out in both directions within the much broader valley as a whole.

"Let's check it out," Martha said, getting out.

Helen, eager to see if Emerson was on the boat, said, "I'm right behind you."

"No," Johns said, killing their excitement. "Stay put in here. I need to check it out first. If anyone's at home, they're aware they've got visitors. Let's do this the safe way."

He got out of the vehicle and tromped down the slope and onto the rattling dock boards. The girls heard his muffled call announcing a police presence and the knock on the door. All was quiet.

"Come on, Helen. There's nobody on board. Let's go see for ourselves."

The girls got out of the vehicle and walked down the slope.

They made it across the rattling boards of the dock and up to the edge of the boat. Martha climbed over first and took Helen's hand to help her over. Helen didn't move. She stood completely still.

"Are you coming?" Martha asked. There, in the pale moonlight, she saw Helen's expression. It was like a sleep walker's, with no movement of the facial muscles to hint at her inner thoughts.

"Helen?" she asked again, but got only a twitch of recognition. Martha tugged on her arm.

"Martha!" Helen exclaimed.

"What?" Martha replied, completely taken aback by Helen's weirdness.

"Did you see her?"

"See who?"

"The ghost. The woman standing right beside you. She wants us to go inside. She's gone," Helen said in a voice raw with awe.

Goose flesh crept all over Martha's skin, like she'd been stung from above. She scrambled back over the boat's railing to stand next to Helen and stare back at the empty deck.

Johns came out from the cabin. Seeing Helen and Martha, he put his hands on his hips in a gesture of hopelessness and said sarcastically, "Didn't want to stay in the car? Thought it would be more fun to live life dangerously and wander around a haunted boat."

"Haunted. Why did you say that of all things right now?" Martha asked.

The Chief's eyebrows furrowed. "What do you mean?"

"You just said 'haunted boat.' What makes you think it's haunted?" Martha pushed forward, excited by the idea the boat might harbor a ghost.

Johns shook his head. "I meant it must have gotten here somehow, but I'm not finding any signs of life, Martha. It was a low attempt at explaining an oddity of the situation."

"We saw two children bring the boat down, remember? But get ready for the real clincher, Helen saw a ghost, Merriam."

"Uh huh? Well, it's been a long night, Martha, and we're all tired."

"I didn't imagine it and I want to go inside," Helen said in a placid tone and so sure of herself, that as she stepped onto the boat and made her way to the cabin entrance, neither Johns nor Martha tried to stop her progress.

Once inside, Helen sat down at the banquet sitting area. Martha came in and sat beside her.

"You doing okay, buddy?" Martha asked in a soft, motherly way.

"I am. There's something here, Martha. I'm trying to wrap my head around it."

Johns stood in the doorway. "Have you made yourselves comfortable? The children aren't here. I want you two back in the car while I go look for Emerson."

"I'm not leaving, yet," Helen said resolutely. "I need to stay for a few minutes longer."

Martha and Johns exchanged "your friend/my friend is a bit touched" looks.

"Stay here, girls. I'm going to look for Emerson." The Chief went up on deck.

"Let's have a light so we can see better." Pointing to the overhead lamp, Martha stood up and inspected the old oil Tiffany fixture. "My grandmother had one of these hanging over her kitchen dining table. It's been a long time, but I think I remember how these like to be treated. Hey, this lamp is warm. It's been recently lit."

"Must have been the children," Helen mused.

As the flame took hold on the wick, the two tired souls stared up into the flickering light and watched how it illuminated the multicolored pieces of glass. Martha tapped a soft beat on the table top with one of her newly painted fingernails.

Glancing repeatedly up at the light and back down at Martha's tapping nail, Helen uttered a firm, "Yes. That has to be it. Since the day I met Stephan, something about these boats has needled me. Their names. Your nail polish reminded me of enamel and enamel reminded me of cloisonné."

Helen continued, "I know you don't believe me, but I saw a woman standing on this boat. What if she was trying to tell me something?"

She fiddled around with the lamp turning it and peering up into its interior.

"What are you doing?" Martha asked, curious.

Helen stopped and sat down. "A few years ago, there was a magazine article, I can't remember who did it, but it was about the lost Fabergé eggs. The listed eggs had unusual names. What if those eggs were on these boats?"

"What do you think this woman was trying to tell you?" Martha asked.

"I'm beginning to think I'm crazy, but if you must know. I think she wanted me to come inside this boat and sit at this table."

They scanned the room for a likely answer. The table was quaint and the booth cushions were fairly new. Nothing about the galley was extraordinary in any way except the beautiful hanging Tiffany-styled light lit above them.

"Oh, my God!" Helen exclaimed peering up into the lamp. "Give me a hand, Martha. See if you can find another light source. I want to take the lamp apart."

Digging in drawers of the Galley kitchen, Martha found some matches and a nice sized candle sitting on the counter. She lit it and brought it over to the table.

Carefully they removed the shade and blew out the wick's flame. Helen unscrewed the extremely large bottom section of the lamp where the oil was contained.

Once dismantled, they put the lamp's bottom half on the galley table. Helen showed Martha where there appeared to be two separate sections connected together. With the right manipulation, the pieces neatly slid apart to reveal one part where the oil was housed and another equally-sized section with a minuscule hole only big enough for a pin to fit into.

"Do you have something to push in the opening?" Helen asked.

Martha went over to the kitchen area and found a metal shish kabob skewer and handed it to her. Gently inserting the pointed end into the tiny hole, the delicate door opened revealing packed insulation. With tentative fingers, Helen pulled out the protective material. Tucked into the back, something glittered.

Pushing her entire hand into the opening, her fingers wrapped around an oval yet rough-textured item. She pulled the hidden treasure from its metal cave. Once in the light, the exquisite beauty of the thing revealed itself.

With a trembling hand and voice, Helen said, "If I'm right, Martha, this is a Fabergé egg missing since the Romanov's lost their throne. Sharon suspected something, too, about the names of the boats and she was killed because of it."

For at least a minute, they marveled at the sheer magnificence of the beautiful, jewel-encrusted egg. Not more than seven inches tall and five inches around, it had lain wrapped and tucked into the family's heirloom lamp for almost a hundred years.

"It's worth millions, Martha. We need to get it to a bank or the constabulary's vault. Put it in your bag, but be so gentle."

Martha wrapped the egg with her sweater and tucked it into her bag. "We better keep it quiet we have it. Let's tell Merriam, that is, if we can find him."

Martha pulled back the curtain covering the window. Something outside arrested her attention. "There's a small figure, Helen, running down the pasture to the boat. It might be Emerson. Good! There goes Merriam walking towards it."

CHAPTER 36

PERIGRINE, HAVING SEEN THE POLICE vehicle, knew Emerson would be safe if he ran the rest of the way to the vehicle.

"I'm going to wait right here, Emerson, to make sure you get to the car. I've got to go back and check on my friend. I can see there are lights on inside the boat. Chief Johns is there and if you run right to him, I owe you an ice cream. Okay?"

"You've got a deal," Emerson said with true childhood joy.

Perigrine scanned the pasture one more time and saw the all-too-familiar silhouette of the Chief stomping around on the boat's deck.

"There he is, Emerson. Get on your way. It's going to take you a few minutes to make it over the distance and down the slope, but you can do it. Don't turn back. Go straight for the Chief."

The young boy took off sprinting, but stopped and turned back to Peregrine. "I didn't get to say thank you. What is your name?"

Perigrine's green eyes twinkled. A thought occurred to him. "It's the Fox and you're welcome. Get going and don't stop."

The child smiled, waved and ran his best through the dew-covered long grass to the boat and safety.

Once the boy was half-way to his goal, Perigrine returned to the spot where he'd left Alistair. With the moon in its zenith, he was able to make out some definite shapes. There on top of a boulder sat Alistair. Perigrine slowed his run to a stroll and approached the thoughtful Al.

"Comfortable? Where are the two hacks?"

"Back there about twenty-feet."

"Asleep?"

"You can call it that, if you want, but more like in need of a few weeks in hospital."

Alistair was quiet for a few minutes and Perigrine didn't push. "This has been fun tonight, P., old pal, but we aren't any closer to getting our nest eggs are we? Where's Emerson?"

"Well, what do you want to hear, the good news or the bad news first?"

"Always the bad news first," Alistair replied.

"The bad news is Chief Johns is on the narrowboat we just left. The good news is Emerson is safe. What should we do with the two hulks lying on the grass over there?"

"Hmm. I don't think we need to worry about it. Here comes the cavalry."

Alistair, from atop his perch, pointed at the two riders crossing the pasture on their right with a massive dog in the lead.

"Let's get up into the trees and watch the excitement from the comfort of a limb," Perigrine said. They climbed fast into the branches of an old oak tree still full with its golden leaves.

"Watch this," Alistair said putting his hands together in the shape of a megaphone, he called out, "Hey! Over here! Come on, help yell."

Together they hooted and hollered until they heard the beating of the horses' hooves on the ground getting closer.

Soon they were grateful they'd climbed the distance from earth to branch. Kaiser came bounding through the grass followed in the distance by the two horses and riders. At first, the German Shepherd sniffed the two unconscious men and stalked around the perimeter of the area as if he believed there was more to the picture than it appeared, but as the riders approached, he went over and waited.

Piers and Sam jumped down and walked over to the two men lying quietly on the ground neatly bound and unconscious.

"These men have been badly beaten," Piers said. "They've got zip ties around their ankles and wrists."

Sam inspected the men. He bent down to check for a pulse. "They're alive." He scanned the area. "Why would anyone tie them up?"

"Don't release them, Sam. They shouldn't be here and Kaiser knew it before any of us. The way they're bound and laid out so neatly, it feels like someone has given them as a…gift."

"Damn right, they're a gift," Alistair muttered, barely audible next to Perigrine who nudged him to be quiet.

"Those two aren't going anywhere. Call Chief Johns, and if you will wait for him to get here, Sam, I'm going on to the dock to find Emerson."

Piers headed to the boat. Sam took out his cell phone and dialed the Chief's number while Perigrine and Alistair were wishing they hadn't climbed the tree after all.

Scene Break

HELEN AND MARTHA HAVING SEEN the shadowy figure of a small child coming through the pasture, jumped up and dashed out of the narrowboat's cabin. Johns called to the boy barely visible in the tall grass.

Emerson waved and called to Johns just as a gunshot rang out and shattered the night's beauty into breathless horror.

The child fell forward into the long grass and Johns shot off in a run toward the spot yelling at Martha and Helen to get back inside the boat. Helen saw Piers on horseback riding fast in their direction. Another shot whizzed past where Helen and Martha stood. They hurried into the boat and scrambled under the galley table. Clinging together they resembled a yin yang symbol.

"Oh, please let Emmy be safe," Helen prayed, her voice raspy.

Martha, too, repeatedly murmured her entreaty for the child's protection. Soon another plink and thud sound indicated another gunshot striking the boat's outer wall.

"Someone's not after Emerson, Helen. They're trying to kill us or maybe just you. Either way, it's not good. I'm about to start shooting back," Martha said angrily. "Why are they after you?"

Able to see with the one eye not squeezed shut and free to open because it wasn't mashed against Martha's cranium, Helen said, "They want the egg. Albright must have known all along Sharon contacted me. Maybe he thought she told me where the eggs were hidden. He didn't want me to get to them first. Did you bring the gun?"

Martha unclamped one hand from their huddled position and reached for her bag on the banquet. She grabbed it and pulled out the neat Ballester-Molina handgun Polly had given her at the farm earlier that day.

"I thought you said this was in your trunk?" Helen squeaked.

"I lied. Do you really want to discuss my veracity issues at this very moment?"

"Do you know how to use it?"

"I do. My daddy taught me. If anyone comes on this boat that isn't friend, he's foe, and I'm shooting his kneecaps out," Martha said, checking the gun to make sure it was ready to fire.

"Good! If someone hurt that child, I might shoot something else off. That is if you'll show me how to fire the gun," Helen offered.

"Tell you what, you focus on dialing your cell phone and getting the rest of the police force over here and I'll watch the door. No one messes with two Southern women and their kids."

A loud thump on the upper deck made the girls reestablish their grips on each other.

Martha whispered, "I need to keep my arm free in case I need to aim, okay?"

Helen nodded in the affirmative and they both became still and small under the table.

The door opened and since no once announced themselves like Johns or Piers would have done, Martha knew it wasn't friend, but foe she was dealing with. Taking a deep breath and letting it out slowly and quietly, she waited. The gun was cocked and ready. Nothing to do, but wait for the lower half of a body to round the corner of the booth.

"Ladies, I think you've got something I want," a man's voice said threateningly. "I've got a gun so let's not play any games, shall we?"

Martha didn't recognize the voice at all, but Helen tugged firmly on her arm.

"Albright," Helen mouthed silently.

As the first knee rounded the corner, Martha set her jaw and steadied her gun hand on her lap. The best advice she'd ever received regarding what to do when forced into a deadly corner with a man twice your size and twice as lethal, was to fire first and ask questions later. That's what Martha did. Aiming at Albright's leg, she pumped a bullet into his thigh.

The noise was deafening. The force of the shot pushed Albright back against the wall and he screamed.

"You crazy bi*#$!," he yelled.

"I'd shut my trap, if I were you," Martha said coolly. "That is unless you want me to shoot a little in the middle next."

Albright tried to move to get hold of the girls, but the wound in his leg was too much for him. He collapsed back against the wall and passed out.

The girls extracted themselves from their hole by squirming up unto the booth seats and maneuvering around the banquet until they were in the clear and near the cabin door.

"Hurry! Let's get Merriam. I'm feeling kind of shaky. I don't want him to die or anything," Martha said, experiencing a small amount of shooter's remorse.

Once on deck and in the crisp autumn night air, they yelled at the top of their lungs for help. There on the horizon, Martha scanned the landscape near the tree line and there was Piers with Emerson wrapped in a blanket.

"I think he's okay, Helen. See?" She pointed out the figures.

"I do. Thank God! But where is Johns?"

"I don't see him…anywhere. Oh, Helen," she said frightened, "do you think he was shot?"

They disembarked and ran over the creaking dock to the pasture. Searching in the wet grass, they called, "Merriam!"

"I'm over here!" came a voice down the side of the river's embankment.

The girls ran over to peer down one of the steep sides where the river had cut a high wall into the ground. Down in the mud and silt struggled the Chief, bloody and tangled in the roots and grasses growing on the precarious edge.

"Merriam!" Martha cried. "I'm getting someone. Hold on!"

"Thanks, I'll do that!" he called back. "Sounds like a good idea! Where's the man who pushed me?"

"He's been shot, but I'm hoping he's not dead…yet."

"Shot! By who?"

Johns went limp and groaned. "Please, please tell me it wasn't you, Martha."

She turned to Helen and shrugged. "Please go get help. Tell them to bring a rope and a stretcher."

"Be right back."

Helen ran up to the slope and soon Sam, Piers and the incredibly strong Kaiser were working to bring Johns back up to terra firma.

Perigrine and Alistair worked their way, under the cover of darkness, to where their jet skis were stowed. Once sirens could be heard coming loudly across the bridge and down the pasture to the docks, two humming engines made their way unnoticed back up the lazy River Calder.

CHAPTER 37

A LARGE GROUP OF PEOPLE congregated near the narrowboat. Johns and the girls, along with a host of police officers, waited for Albright to be brought out of the boat. Helen explained to Johns that the man inside was the Albright she'd known in Nottingham and Martha remembered him from the day at Polly's farm as one of the police officers who helped to chase away the thugs in the barn. The medical emergency team was inside the boat preparing to bring him out on a stretcher.

"So it was Albright all this time," Helen said to Johns. "Chief, I'd like to show you something."

She pulled the lovely nephrite and diamond Fabergé egg from Martha's bag. "It's about this. If my guess is right, there should be two more. Individually they're worth twenty to thirty million dollars. Together, I can't even fathom their value."

Johns stood up and came over to the delicate treasure she cradled in her two hands wrapped in a Martha's sweater and stared down at it. Piers, Michael and the other officers gathered around Helen to see, too.

"Where did you find it?" he asked.

"The lamp over the galley table. It's been there for years, ninety or more, I would estimate."

At that moment, the emergency technicians brought Albright out of the boat and loaded him onto a stretcher. Johns walked over to the dock. He motioned for Helen to follow him. The wounded man was coherent and once they carried him across the rattling boards of the dock, Johns signaled for them to stop.

He stood next to the reclined figure. “Richards, or should I call you Albright?”

With a slight groan, Albright replied, “It’s neither.”

“Well, whoever you are, you’ve killed two people and tried for two more all in an attempt to get this.”

Johns waved Helen forward. “Show him, Mrs. Ryes.”

A bit uncertain and keeping her distance, Helen took the egg and unwrapped the sweater. Holding it up for him to see, the moonlight hit the diamonds giving a luminescence to the green nephrite stone making the egg glow and sparkle to the awe of everyone who saw it.

Albright, or whoever he was, sunk with a miserable groan deeper into the stretcher. He covered his eyes with his arm and turned his head away.

“I want his hands checked for residue and get him to the hospital. He needs to be alive when we convict him of double homicide and intent to kill Mrs. Ryes and Mrs. Littleword,” Johns said to the EMTs.

Turning to everyone still standing around, he said, “We’re all tired, but safe. I need statements. Afterwards, you can go home and get some sleep.”

Piers came up, leading his horse with Emerson on the back. Helen went over to them.

“Have you been having a big adventure, Emerson?” she asked, smiling up at the boy.

“Oh, yes! But it was fun and only a little scary.”

The child turned to Piers and realizing a truth, he said excitedly, “You were there, like you said you would be.”

Flinging himself off the horse's back and into Piers' arms, he gave Piers a joyful hug.

Johns walked up. "Is Emerson doing okay?"

Piers was aglow with paternal happiness. With a huge smile, he answered, "He's perfectly fine. The first gunshot startled him and made him fall."

Sam had briefed Johns about the two bound men found in the woods. They, too, had been dealt with neatly, like the men on the boats back in town. It was as if someone was working very efficiently on the side of the police but not coming forward for the credit.

"You're a brave boy, Emerson. How did you manage to get away from those two roughnecks we found in the woods? Did you see anyone else in the woods?" Johns asked.

Emerson fiddled with one of Piers' pockets on his coat and with the simple style of a child responded, "I didn't do anything. It was the Fox who helped me escape."

Johns and Piers exchanged slightly perplexed expressions.

"What did the Fox do? Did it scare the men?" Johns asked, somewhat confused by the response.

"He told me to come to him. I got on his back and we escaped. He showed me where you were and said I should run to you."

The two adults stayed quiet for a few seconds. Johns motioned for Piers to come away for a moment. Piers put Emerson back on top of his horse with Sam holding the bridle. Once at a decent distance, Johns said, "Children often times align their frightening experiences with something comforting or known to them. It helps them put the situation into a context they understand. He's probably been reading something about a fox or a superhero. Don't worry, he'll be fine."

Piers nodded and said in a low tone, "He's been fascinated with the fox trap and wanting to set the fox loose. I'm sure that has something to do with it."

"Oh, one more thing," Emerson yelled toward the Chief and Piers.

"What?" Piers called back.

"The Fox promised me ice cream."

Johns and Piers turned back around to each other and smiled knowingly. With a shared chuckle, they walked back to the spot where Emerson chatted with Helen and Martha.

"I'll buy you some ice cream, Emerson. You can count on it," Helen said.

After the statements were finished, everyone departed to their respected homes for a much-needed sleep. Johns sent every available officer to guard the last two Rossar-mescro boats still tethered down below The Traveller's Inn. If there were eggs to be found aboard the Blue Hen and the Cherub, he didn't want any sneaky foxes to get to them first.

CHAPTER 38

LATER THAT DAY, MARTHA WOKE from a delicious sleep in her own fluffy bed at Flower Pot Cottage surrounded by Amos, Vera and Gus. For a long time she lay there soaking up the quiet and the warmth of having three furry, curled up rocks positioned on both sides of her.

"Guys, I've missed you so much. It's good to be home."

Her cell phone rang and Martha stretched with difficulty to reach it on the nightstand next to her bed. It was Kate, her daughter, calling.

"Baby!" she trilled with a huge smile across her face. "How are you?"

"I'm fine, Mamma. Have you been taking good care of yourself?" Kate asked.

Kate still called her mother Mamma partly because Martha was stubborn and wouldn't answer to anything else.

Martha crossed her fingers and her legs to ward off any bad mojo from telling a lie and answered, "Nothing exciting happening here. Same old stuff. We've been working on The Grange's collection and we're almost done. When are you coming home for a weekend? I'd love to hear all the gossip from school."

Kate filled Martha in on the happenings at Oxford and told her she would be home at Christmas break, good news for Martha because that meant only another two months or so to wait.

"I'd like to bring a friend for a few days. Would that be okay with you?" Kate asked.

Martha detected something new in her daughter's voice. The way Kate said friend had a different ring to it and although she was dying to know, Martha didn't snoop, but said instead, "You bring home anyone you want, sweetie. I'd love to meet them."

They talked a while longer then said goodbye. She got up and walked out to the stairwell and checked in the guest room only to find an empty bed. Leaning over the banister, she yelled, "Hey, Helen! You awake?"

"Out here!" Helen yelled back. "I'm on the internet."

Helen was deep in the history of the Faberge Easter eggs given to The Empress Maria Feodorovna by both her son, Czar Nicholas II and her husband, Czar Alexander III. They'd been lost to time after the Red Army took over Russia. Most of the eggs were in private museums, private collections or at the Kremlin Armory Museum in Moscow, but a handful of Maria's favorites were unaccounted for.

Martha toddled downstairs followed by her menagerie and after the furry dependents were fed, watered and let outside for some fresh air, she sat down by Helen and read over her shoulder about how a handful of the Romanov Faberge eggs were still considered lost.

"Do any of the ones that are listed as lost resemble the one you found?" Martha asked.

Helen replied with an awed excitement in her voice, "Yes. The name of the boat was the key. We were on the Empire and one of the eggs belonging to Maria Feodorovna given to her by her husband was designed in the Empire style."

"Do you think it's the same?" Martha asked.

Turning to Martha, Helen took a deep breath and let it out. "I think the egg we found has been inside that lamp for an extremely long time. The Rossar-mescros will hopefully be able to give us more of the story. It's so exciting, Martha, I can hardly stand it."

"Well, one thing's for sure, The Rossar-mescros are going to be rich beyond their wildest dreams."

Scene Break

TWO DAYS LATER, IN A PETIT bistro neatly placed on a corner of rue Saint-Séverin in Paris, sat two dapper Englishmen, drinking XO Cognac and reading an english version of the French evening paper, Le Monde. They'd been comfortably tucked into one of the discrete corner booths for over an hour. Only the occasional attendance of the waiter, who'd been paid to stay aloof but keep a watchful eye on their tulip glasses' levels, compelled them to speak, if only to say merci.

"I wouldn't mind visiting Frank while we're here," Perigrine said, swirling the amber spirit hypnotically inside the curvy shaped glass.

"He won't be here this time of year. It's the rodeo season in Oregon and he never misses the women's barrel racing competitions." Alistair raised his eyebrows. "Frank likes powerful women manipulating large animals."

"Too bad. I always enjoy his Blanquette de Veau. For an Italian from Queens, he's an amazing French cook."

Perigrine, finished with his paper, tossed it over to the other table and let out a sigh. "That was a ghost on that boat, Alistair. You don't want to believe what your eyes saw but she wanted to tell us something."

"Well, I'm not one for ignoring a good tip, P. I've been checking out the word Mavia, we heard the Romani boy call that night."

"Not the boy," Perigrine said shaking his head back and forth.

"Boy. Definitely, the boy," Alistair said firmly. "Anyway, Mavia sounds a lot like Mauve, don't you think?"

Perigrine mused a little bit. "Yes, indeed it does. A name and a missing boat, what do you make of it?"

"It so happens that before you got here, I made a call to Stephan Rossar-mescro to check on names in his family. Seems Mavia is written in the family bible as the mother of Sophia Rossar-mescro, the ancestor who purchased the two narrowboats."

"Where's the Mavia boat then? Or for that matter, where's the fourth egg mentioned in the letter? Did she sell it to buy the two boats?"

"Perhaps but that's the interesting part. There is an inner piece referred to as 'the surprise' fitting that description which turned up over eighty years ago and was sold at a London auction but the egg it's known to belong to never surfaced."

"Where could it be?" Perigrine asked while sipping from his glass.

"We might consider she had it buried with her, but when I asked Stephan where Sophia was interred, he said she'd purchased an expensive burial plot in one of London's most famous cemeteries."

"Brompton?"

"You got it. She bought three plots at Brompton in fact. One for herself, one for her husband and, get ready for it. One for her mother, Malvia."

"Good, lord, Alistair. You're a genius. Did you say anything to Stephan?"

"No. If the egg is there, it needs to be collected by MI5 once we talk to Val. That is if she ever gets here."

"She'll be here. She's being cautious…and a bit vindictive as usual. Valerie likes to make people wait. It's her way of paying it forward, so to speak." Perigrine adjusted his Burberry tie.

The tinkling of a bell let them know someone had entered the bistro. Soon a fascinating and extremely potent aroma like vanilla caramel and cotton candy wafted into the back room where Perigrine and Alistair waited for the physical to catch up with the promise. Alistair shifted his right leg onto his left, an imperceptible indication of his inner frame of mind. It didn't go unnoticed by P.

A tall, excruciatingly slim woman in her late thirties, walked with poise into the room. She wore a bright, hot pink form-fitting dress and a cropped black jacket, black tights and hot pink ankle boots. Her brown hair was twisted up into a neat bun and her skin had never seen a full dose of sun without proper protection. It was still in its original creaminess she'd been blessed with from her English mother.

Sitting down beside Alistair, she leaned over and brushed her lips across his cheek whispering, "Hello, Ally." She drew out the last word as she gave Perigrine a smoldering gaze. "You're scrumptious as ever. Too bad you brought that old, tired thing with you."

Looking Perigrine up and down skeptically, she pursed her crimson lips in a note of displeasure. "And you're…tidy, P.P."

Perigrine rolled his eyes heavenward and with a pause for effect, he retorted, "Is that crow's feet around your eyes, Valerie, or the accumulated weathering of your years as a tart?"

Valerie gave Alistair a firm squeeze right above his knee, causing him to stiffen. Her pouty, red lips curved into a sweet smile as she focused all her attention on Alistair's ear. "Do you hear that pathetic buzzing sound, Ally? I think it must be a dirty, little fly or something even more parasitic. I don't know why you keep the old thing around."

"That's it! Alistair," Perigrine said hotly. "I'm going to Notre Dame. Call me when you're done with her."

He stood up regally and slipping on his long, camel-colored trench coat, he walked out saying, "You deal with good old Val, Alistair. I'll see you later."

As the door's bell signaled Perigrine's exit, Valerie leaned in again and put her head on Alistair's shoulder with a sigh.

"I'm so glad he's gone. He's such a prig. Missed me much?" she asked.

Alistair patted her on the top of her head. "You're enjoying yourself, Val, but teasing Perigrine this way will not change his feelings. If you would, please let the blood flow resume again in my leg and sit up. Let's talk about your little problem with Ken Young or as he likes to call himself, Thomas Albright."

Valerie sighed and readjusted herself in the booth. She didn't completely disengage herself from trying to become a carbuncle on Alistair's left arm, but she did stop the heavy breathing and slowed the thigh squeezing.

"Oh Ally, it's been such a terrible week. If I tell you what you want to know, I'll probably end up like that woman they found in the canal." She breathed into his ear. "That would be such a shame when I still have so much to offer."

Again she snuggled up closer to Alistair who, using his free arm, waived at the waiter to bring another snifter.

"Val, the police have Albright. He'll throw you to the dogs. With the people he's got things on, he's sure to go free and he'll come back for you, and possibly Helen."

The woman squirmed in her seat and released her tension on Alistair's arm, allowing the blood to flow again. She fiddled with the tulip glass the waiter had sat in front of her with Cognac.

"Mine?" she asked.

"Naturally."

"How did you know it was me who carried the shashka to the London dealer?"

"Perigrine talked with the dealer. You may share the same hair color as Helen Ryes, but once he described the perfume, it was game up for you. He said it was the one thing that really stood out and unfortunately for you, he actually recognized the scent's elements. Helen Ryes wears Coco by Chanel not Angel by Thierry Mugler.

She swirled the liquid around in the bottom of the glass and took a slow sip. Turning to Alistair, Valerie said with slight worry, "I'm not kidding, Ally, they'll kill me if I talk. I owed Young a favor from a few years ago. He caught me with my hand in the cookie jar, so to speak and arranged my return from Kiev." Val sat quiet for a few seconds and took another sip of the Cognac. "I only came when you called because I wanted to see Perigrine."

The two sat for a little longer. After a moment of quiet contemplation, Alistair said, "Go on, Val. He told you where he was going. Go make up. Be nice and not so waspish." Then after a pause, he added, "Do me a favor?"

She stood up and smoothed her dress. "What?"

"I know it was you they used to frame Helen Ryes. Young will serve his time for murdering Sharon O'Connor and Laura Rossar-mescro only if you come forward. You're the glue that proves it was for gain and that Young was the mastermind behind it. The four thugs won't dare talk. It's two deaths and you know who did it. Come clean. I'll see to it the Russians he was working for never find you."

Val bent down and cupped Alistair's face in her hands. "Ally, you have the most beautiful eyes I've ever seen on a man." Kissing him long and slowly on his mouth, once done, she dropped her hands and picked up her purse. She dug around and pulled out a pretty blue bottle of perfume which she opened and dabbed at her wrists and neck. The room filled with the heady fragrances of Bergamot, Caramel, and Patchouli. There was an undefined innocence in what she said next.

"It's funny. I've always liked the idea of marriage. I would feel so safe living in a small cottage somewhere in Yorkshire. Want to make an honest woman of me, Alistair?" With a last wink, she turned and made for the door.

Alistair didn't watch her go. He knew, if she decided to talk, she wouldn't announce it here. He picked up his own coat and slipping it on, he, too, strolled out, causing the tiny bell above the door to jangle for the third and last time that night.

CHAPTER 39

JOHNS, PIERS, POLLY AND THE girls sat in one of The Traveller's coziest booths right across from the fireplace, well-laid with logs causing the fire to make crackling and popping sounds comforting to the human ear. They were going over the crazy night from a couple of days before.

The regulars were also enjoying their pints and in the back an occasional brouhaha erupted from the dart players. A steady rain, along with a heavy drop in temperature, told the inhabitants of Marsden-Lacey and all of Northern England that autumn was in her fullness.

Johns was explaining what they'd found on the other two boats while the rest of the party squeezed in close to hear every word.

"We found two more eggs in the same place: the galley lamps. I want to take you over tomorrow to London to see them. They were picked up yesterday by three armored cars and as many security vans sent for additional protection. They'll be six stories down in a facility so secure an atom bomb couldn't blow the door."

"What will happen to Albright, or whoever he is?" Piers asked.

"That's not his name. His real name is Ken Young, a long-time secret service agent for the CIA. Spent years working as a spy in the Ukraine. He's a nasty fellow and has strong ties to the Russian mob. Not an ounce of humanity left in him."

"Did he kill Sharon?" Helen asked softly.

"He didn't commit the murder, but he had Victor, "The Dove", do the work. Victor's fingerprints were the ones found on the shashka that killed Laura Rossar-mescro. They also found traces of skin under Sharon's fingernails matching Victor's DNA. Albright, I mean Young, was the brains. He managed to set himself up with a fake police identification and pay off someone in Nottingham's office to fax a phony request for collaboration between our two constabularies. His entire goal was to have access to everything we were doing on the case so he would know when it was best to send his men in to find the eggs."

"Will he serve a sentence?" Martha asked.

"As for a sentence, that's tricky. It'll depend on evidence and getting a statement from someone who took orders from him. We're looking for the woman who traded the cossack's shashka which killed Laura for the diamond necklace. None of the men he had working for him will point the finger at him. They're either connected with the Russian mafia or too afraid to talk. There for a while, Helen, things were looking kind of bad for you, but now I'd love it if you'd turn evidence on Albright, Young or whatever his real name is."

"What makes you think I'm not guilty?" Helen asked with a good natured smile.

"You were with Piers having tea at the same time the woman who pawned the shashka came into the antique store in London. Can't be two places at once."

Piers winked at Helen and said, "You owe me one."

Helen nudged him with her elbow. "Hush."

Johns went on with his story. “Ballistics matched the gun Albright-Young used to fire at Helen and Martha on the narrowboat with the bullets found imbedded in the boat’s outer walls. He had gunpowder residue on his hands. It will be up to Helen and Martha to testify about his threatening them in the boat.”

“What about Martha plugging him in the leg?” Helen asked with a laugh.

“Better him than us,” Martha replied.

“She’ll have to account for why she had the gun in the first place and why she used it. That’s the law. Might even get to lock her up for a while.”

“Don’t get your hopes up, Merriam. I have a good solicitor. She told me not to discuss my case with the police.”

Everyone laughed.

“Did he kill Sharon for the letter?” Helen asked.

“Definitely,” Johns replied. “She must have contacted him about it. They would have known of each other living in the same town and even Helen was aware of his expertise in the field of translations.”

“I’d known of Albright for at least ten years. He lived in Nottingham and worked as a translator for at least as long. Our paths didn’t cross much, but other colleagues talked about his work,” Helen said.

“Sharon’s email was finally opened. In it, the real Nottingham police found correspondence sent to Albright the day before she was found floating in the canal. She’d only copied half the letter and requested his translation of it.”

"He realized the incredible truth of what Ivan Ivovich, the Cossack of Maria Feodorovna, had written in the letter. His email back to Sharon requested to see more of the letter. She may have been threatened later or simply killed outright."

"He ought to be publicly strung up," Martha said then sipped her drink.

"I agree," Polly added with a big smile and raised her glass to Martha.

"You, two, simmer down. No toasting each other. We know where that got you the last time," Helen said severely.

Martha and Polly ignored her and clinked glasses anyway.

"What about the Rossar-mescros? Don't the eggs belong to them?" Piers asked.

"That's where it gets sticky. They actually belong to the Empress Dowager and her descendants and after talking with Stephan earlier, he wants to do the right thing."

Martha reached over to pick up one of the brie topped crackers they'd ordered for appetizers and asked, "Was he shocked to know they'd been inside the lamps all this time?"

Johns didn't get a chance to answer because a gentle voice interrupted their huddled conversation. Looking up, they all fell quiet. There stood Stephan Rossar-mescro himself, smiling sweetly and holding his tatty, brown fedora in his two hands.

"Good evening," Stephan said.

"Mr. Rossar-mescro," Helen said, standing up to greet him, "How are you?"

"I am fine, thank you dear lady. We're leaving for our home waters and I wanted to thank you for all you've done. There is some good news I wanted to share with all of you."

The group waited, giving him their full attention.

He continued. "After I finished with our talk, Chief Johns, I called the man you told me to, the Director for Her Majesty's Royal Collection. He invited me and a guest to London. He wants to see the eggs and to discuss a settlement."

Everyone at the table offered him their congratulations.

Johns said, "Mr. Rossar-mescro, we're so happy to hear your good news."

"Yes, and if you need any help, please don't be afraid to ask," Helen offered with a kind touch on his shoulder.

"There is one thing, Mrs. Ryes, I would ask of you." Stephan said shyly.

"Name it."

Mr. Rossar-mescro appeared nervous and unsure of his request. He said in an awed voice, "I have been asked to meet Her Majesty, The Queen."

Everyone at the table exclaimed their happiness and wished him a wonderful time.

"This is my request, I would like to take Mrs. Ryes with me, if she will come. They'll want to talk about the eggs and I would feel honored to have such a beautiful and intelligent woman at my side to give me courage."

Helen took the gentle man's hand and with eyes glassy from unshed tears she said, "I would love to accompany you, Mr. Rossar-mescro. It would be a dream come true. Thank you."

He blushed and, with a cheerful wave to all, left promising to contact Helen as soon as the date was set for the Royal visit.

"I guess you know he's got a thing for you, Helen." Piers said.

"Maybe, but what a first date!" she said, jabbing Piers in the side.

With no attempt at retaining her usual composure, Helen reached across the table, grabbed Martha's two hands, and shaking them with vigor said in a gleeful squeal, "I'm going to meet The Queen! Can you believe it, Martha? Isn't it crazy?"

Laughing and squeezing Helen's hands in return, Martha answered, "Crazy as a fox, buddy. Crazy as a fox!"

CHAPTER 40

THREE WEEKS LATER, A MEETING was arranged between a slim, brunette woman and the Crown Prosecution Services regarding a man she knew as Ken Young alias Thomas Albright. The two parties discussed a business arrangement regarding the delivery of a long, curved sword or shashka, to an antique dealer in London. In return for her testimony, she would be given immunity and relocated to a new place under a new name. She returned the diamond necklace as proof of her involvement.

That same week, Helen and Martha went to London where Helen did attend a press conference regarding the unprecedented find of three Fabergé eggs once belonging to the Romanovs of Imperial Russia. She was later invited along with Mr. Rossar-mescro to attend a private audience with The Queen and a host of other dignitaries who previewed the first major exhibition of Fabergé eggs in the Royal Collection.

Martha, Chief Johns, Piers and Emerson took in the sights of the most beloved capital of the English speaking world, London. With Tallant Rossar-mescro, Stephan's grandson, in tow, the promise of ice cream and treats Emerson wrangled from Celine was fulfilled at Harrod's Ice Cream Parlour. Later, with Helen acting as docent, the entire group visited the Fabergé exhibition, marveling at the three eggs nearly lost to time.

After leaving Paris, Perigrine and Alistair took a much-needed holiday to Majorca where they visited some old friends and chartered a small sail boat to visit some of the nearby smaller islands.

Having broken the mystery explaining where the last of the four Fabergé eggs had been secreted, they worked out a lucrative deal. The Mavia, or Mauve egg, would be going home to the Russian people as a gift from the British government, that is as long as Valerie Clark, Perigrine's sister, was allowed to live a peaceful life secure from reprisals.

Where did they find the remaining Mauve egg not connected to a boat in any way? Sophia Rossar-mescro, in order to purchase the two narrowboats for her family, sold the heart-shaped piece which nestled inside the Mauve egg. The first three eggs: the Cherub, the Empire and the Blue Hen, became the good-luck totems for the families' boats and were secreted inside the Tiffany style lamps specially constructed for the galleys.

The Mauve egg was found in a place powerful with meaning for the young Romani girl, Sophia, who lost her mother and her sister in a bomb explosion during World War One. Instead of putting the egg somewhere in the boats, she'd placed the egg as a testimony in an hallowed place, Brompton Cemetery, befitting her mother's legacy.

The lost treasures of Maria Feodorovna and the quest of Ivan Ivovich Lysenko, her faithful Cossack, had come full circle. The Rossar-mescros returned three of the eggs and the Mauve egg was retrieved by the Director of MI5 two days after Valerie Clark left for a quiet retreat in Palm Springs, California.

Miri Rossar-mescro's prophecy was finally complete.

"A Helen holds the letter.
A hunter wields the blade.
Death creeps among us,
A debt is finally paid."

Thank you for reading!

If you'd like to enjoy Helen and Martha's continuing journey, check out

Pudding, Poison & Pie available in Amazon's Kindle Unlimited program.

About the Author

Sigrid Vansandt lives with her husband, daughter and small maltipoo, Amos, in the Ozarks of Arkansas.

She always wanted to write and with the encouragement of her family finally gave it a try. An avid reader of all things British and the American South, she enjoyed combining the two cultures into her first cozy mystery series.

Thank you for reading!

Email Sigrid at: sigridvansandt@gmail.com